JACK OF SPADES

A Jack of All Trades novel

DH Smith

to Jenny
I hope you like this
book too!
DH Smith

Earlham Books

Published 2015 by Earlham Books
Book design & cover art by Lia at Free Your Words
(*www.FreeYourWords.com*)

ISBN: 978-1-909804-15-9

PART ONE:
THE CAST & SETTING

Chapter 1

A mid chunk of the wall had toppled like a sideways domino, crushing the flower bed, the top broken onto the edge of the lawn. The rest of the wall leaned dangerously, all the way from the house to the high fence at the back of the garden, as if it had been pushed by a giant's boot. The brickwork was a dirty yellow, pitted and lumpy like bread pudding. There were tired flowers along its length, some white and red chrysanthemums, funeral flowers he thought. Was that a dahlia clump? And other plants, sad green islands past their flowering. On the wall itself was a gnarled climber, with a few scattered orange roses braving the October wind.

Jack had already spoken to the family next door, telling them he'd need to go into their garden too. The old lady had asked him to be careful of the flowers and he'd told her that with the way the wall was leaning, most of the demolished bricks wouldn't go into their garden at all. It was the gripe of garden jobs; always someone saying take care of my flowers, keep off the lawn. And then coming out to watch you, but honestly, how can you take a wall down and look after flowers too? He was going to clobber the brickwork with a sledgehammer; he wouldn't be taking fairy steps to mind the irises. He had a club hammer and cold chisel, in addition, to get him started in various places, but the bricks would fall where the bricks would fall.

He'd start with the fallen length and break it up into manageable bits, then wheelbarrow it out to the skip he had in the road outside. Then go for the wall still standing on either side of the gap. He adjusted his safety goggles, never liked them, they irritated his nose and brow, and took the sledgehammer and gloves out of the barrow just as a woman came out of the house.

Here we go.

He shoved the goggles up onto his forehead as she approached. She was youngish, mid 20s perhaps, skinny in a shapeless dress that came below her knees. She had a distressed look and he knew she was coming to claim ownership of the flowerbed. He smiled as she came close; she had a timidity about her, the way she was chewing her nails.

A couple of metres away, on the edge of the lawn, she stopped. She was wearing plastic trainers and no socks. Her skin was sallow, too white, her hair straight and lank. She was trembling, breathing quickly.

'Hello,' he said, to help her out. 'Do you live here?'

She nodded and smiled through a mouth of yellow and grey teeth, gaps here and there.

'You the builder?' she said in a quiet, squeaky voice.

'I am,' he said. It was a too obvious question, but he felt a joke at her expense would shrivel her like a spinach leaf in hot water. 'I'm taking down this wall. About to fall down by itself anyway. Then I'm replacing it with a wooden fence. Hope to finish by the end of the week.'

'They're my flowers,' she said, indicating the flowerbed along the length of the distressed wall.

Jack sighed. 'I've got to knock the wall down, there's bound to be some damage.' He could see tears welling in her eyes. They were very blue and she seemed about to collapse herself. 'I'll be as careful as I can but you can't be delicate with a sledgehammer and falling bricks.'

She nodded, wiping her eyes with the back of her hand. 'If I prune the roses, then...'

'That would be a great idea,' he said over enthusiastically. 'A real hard prune. I was wondering how to deal with them.'

'They're old,' she said, 'but I do love that orange colour. It's the same as nasturtiums. They've been here all my life.

My mum planted them when she and Dad first moved in, before I was born.'

'Tell your mum, I'll be as careful as I can.'

'She's dead.'

'I'm sorry,' he said.

'Ten years ago now. I told her I would look after her flowerbed.'

Jack was feeling distinctly uncomfortable, he didn't need her family history. 'I can't take the wall down brick by brick,' he said. 'I've got to clobber it.' He shrugged helplessly.

He watched her eyes, those very blue eyes, and expected a tantrum, the sort of thing his ten year old daughter would do. And then what would he do? Great start to a morning.

Then she surprised him.

'I've got my tools in that shed,' she said, pointing out the structure at the end of the garden. 'Suppose I dig up the plants just before you get to them. You take away the broken bricks, and then I put them back in.'

'You're a very practical young lady,' he said, impressed. 'That's a good plan.' No tantrum, liquid intelligence in those blue eyes.

'Thank you,' she said with her toothy smile, and almost curtseyed. 'Would you like a cup of tea?' Then as an afterthought, 'What's your name?'

Jack had his thermos in his van, but knew better than to say no. The first job of a small builder is to get on with the householders.

'It's Jack,' he said. 'And I'm dying for a cuppa.'

Chapter 2

Anne watched, through the French windows, the silly girl upstairs with the bad teeth. Always around the house. The girl made her angry. Clothes were cheap enough, and there were jumble sales too. Her dress had been washed to a rag, and her hair and those tacky trainers... As if she was determined to make the worst of herself. Anne wasn't expecting her to step out of Vogue, but a little attention to hair and body, a little pride in herself. She could get a better dress for a pound from a charity shop.

Bessie. Why Bessie? Why not Betty or Liz? Bessie sounded like a fat bakery assistant.

Was she chatting up the builder? Not a bad looking guy. Curly brown hair, muscular, almost as if posing with that sledgehammer by his side. Cliché. Nice though. Shirt sleeves rolled up, in paint-flecked, navy overalls. Ready for work. She shook herself. Fantasies. Undo those straps, pull down that bib and get her hands under his shirt...

The baby started crying. She half smiled and shrugged, picking the baby out of the playpen. The smell and lumpiness in the nappy area said changing time. The crying said feed me. Which end should she attend to first?

She glanced at the twins. The girl was splayed out on the carpet, fast asleep, the boy chewing a wooden giraffe. When the girl woke she'd read them the animal book. It bored her soppy, she'd read it so many times, but they loved the noises the book made and her attempts at animal sounds.

Food for this wailing bundle. Shut up the racket. She flicked a finger under his chin and tweaked his nose. The baby without ceasing the clamour pulled his head away. Realising distraction was useless, Anne put him in the highchair, locking him in securely. It was all locks and bolts and halters, this childminding business. Don't let them out of your sight for a second. No wonder she couldn't have an unbroken fantasy. She glanced wistfully out of the window. They were still talking. Surely he didn't fancy her? Though you could never tell with men. Teenagers, children, babies even. How did that work?

Anything they could overpower.

The baby was shaking its fists frantically. She held his cheeks and rubbed her nose against his.

'Just like you,' she said, kissing the tip of his nose. 'Who will you be thumping in twenty years?'

And she left the pugilist, to put a bowl of mush in the microwave.

About time she met someone. She'd endeavour to have a word with the builder. Size him up close to. Might be just a football obsessed thicko but you never know. And she was a little desperate for adult company. The girl was waking up; there'd be a fight soon, they'd both want the giraffe. Feed wailer, then milk and a satsuma for those two. Change ex-wailer.

And so it goes on.

She looked out again at the builder. Bessie had gone. He was togged up, squaring up to hit the fallen wall with his sledgehammer. Strongman stuff. I am paying for you, she thought. Down came the sledgehammer with a mighty thump. Up, and another crack. She watched him pick up a clump of bricks and put it in his wheelbarrow, just as the microwave beeped.

Mustn't forget the meeting tonight, as she took out the mush. To discuss Tarzan's wages, and there was to be a plumber, an electrician, and roofing work too. Two thousand bloody quid was her share. No way, with or without a sledgehammer. She took a sip. Too hot. Wail on, little one, you don't want to burn your tongue.

The fight over the giraffe had begun.

Chapter 3

Nancy had her coat on, the green check one with the big black buttons. Her stick was ready by the front door. Dial-A-Ride should be here in twenty minutes. Should she go to the toilet again? She'd gone twice but you never know. It was horrible to be caught short, you never knew where or when, and toilets had shut almost everywhere. She'd purposely not had breakfast, just a cup of tea, to keep herself empty.

They said they'd ring ten minutes before they got here. She looked at her list again. Should she make it three tins of sardines instead of two? It was all getting so expensive. Sardines were so easy. On toast, with beans, a sandwich. And if she didn't finish a tin, well Tickles would. Where was he, the little rascal?

And that girl. Out there chatting with the builder. She paid her £15 a week to empty the cat litter, put out the bins and just do a few errands. And there she was chatting away, keeping a man from his work – and the cat litter stinking her flat out. One thing she wouldn't begrudge was cat litter. Tickles deserved it. He shouldn't have to do his business over his own mess. He was her pretty boy, sitting in her lap while she watched *Flog It!*, purring like an old fridge.

And the girl's father had kicked him. Can you imagine! She would never have known if she hadn't seen. Tickles had got past her out the door, and was going past him on the stairs when he booted the cat down the steps. A really vicious kick. She'd yelled at him. Keep your dirty animal off the stairs, he'd yelled back. Tickles wasn't dirty. He never messed on the stairs as he hardly ever went out. And what a trouble she'd had getting him back! The man wouldn't help at all. Just yelled, serves you bloody well right. It was the nice lady downstairs had caught Tickles. He might've been run over.

Nancy told Bessie. And Bessie said sorry for her dad. Said she'd tell him, but she knew the girl wouldn't. Frightened of the brute. They say it starts with animals, serial killers, something easy to practise on, then people.

Now she was really careful when she went to the door, keeping Tickles in. He might be passing again. It'd really bruised poor puss's ribs, that kick.

She counted the money in her purse again. £35. Plenty. Oh, that time when she did her shop in Stratford and just had a fiver with her. So embarrassing. She had her credit card and couldn't remember the pin number. She had written it down, but could she find it when she needed it, really needed it? It was only when she left the supermarket that she found it, a screwed up bit of paper at the bottom of her purse. She'd had to leave the shop with nothing, her face burning with the shame of it, all those people fuming in the queue behind her. That week cost her a fortune, she'd had to send Bessie up to the corner shop on Upton Lane where everything cost twice as much.

Ted said, come to Canada, Mum. Oh, fine to say! Where she'd be in the way, know no one. They'd soon get sick of her. At least here she had her bingo and Millie, who was coming tomorrow from Barkingside, if her cold was better. And that girl to do her errands. When she stopped talking to the builder.

At this rate Dial-A-Ride would come before Bessie did, she'd have to go out and then would come back to a flat stinking of cat litter. Stinking even more than now with Tickles having to go on dirty litter. If only she had a balcony or was down on the ground floor, then Tickles could go outside and do his business. But that Anne, the childminder, had the downstairs flat, though she did have children to look after. She'd made her flat really nice, had invited her in when it was finished. The nursery room was lovely. But no,

Nancy wouldn't be moving. Not her time of life. This was where they'd lay her out. All the stuff she had, it gave her palpitations just thinking about furniture vans.

It was difficult having to do everything yourself. Or at least make sure things got done. John had done so much, gone nine years now. They'd argued a lot when he retired. He was always around the house, but then he got into the garden, planting half the patch out there with vegetables. And that was better for both of them. She missed him so much at first, no one here but herself. And Tickles of course. He'd saved her life.

A glance out the window, and yes, Bessie was going in at last. Had finished with the builder. What a gossip that girl was. She'd catch her on the stairs. Nancy grabbed the edge of the sofa and pulled herself along. She'd have to be speedy to catch Bessie, as she always bounced up the stairs so quickly, so noisily for such a slight thing.

Hand on the wall, Nancy took the last few steps to the front door. Next to it lay the stinking tray, the lumps covered, but it was damp and sharp.

Bessie was padding up the stairs. She'd just catch her.

The phone rang.

That'd be Dial-A-Ride. Nancy changed direction. She should have put the handset in her pocket. She was always doing this, leaving it in its block and then having to rush to make it before the ringing stopped. She scrabbled along, holding onto the back of the sofa, then fell to her knees – and continued crawling along the carpet, breathing fast, the footsteps outside padding past her door.

She grabbed the handset. Was it the red or the green button? She was always getting them wrong. Red, no, green. Green for go. She pressed green.

'You are due thousands of pounds in repayment of your payment protection insurance...' began an automated, well-spoken woman's voice.

'No, I'm not, you stupid cow!' she screamed into the

phone and before the automaton could reply, thrust the phone back on its seating.

Nancy sat back on the floor exhausted, a veined hand, covered in kidney blotches, pressed against her lifting chest. These nuisance calls drove her mad. She knew it was stupid to yell at them, but their endless calls, lying messages... How could they possibly know what she had or hadn't?

There was a timid rap on the door.

'It's me, Mrs Home,' came Bessie's voice. 'Come to do the litter.'

'Won't be a minute, darling,' she shouted back, pulling herself to her feet on the arm of the sofa. Resting a second, then drawing herself along the back of the sofa. 'Coming, Bessie love.'

The phone rang again.

Chapter 4

Frank was drinking his tea splayed out in the armchair, his feet on a wooden chair. He'd undone the laces in his shoes. One hand was on the mound of his stomach as if trying to press in the pie from his rest stop that morning at the tea halt at Whipps Cross pond. He'd undone his belt, the zip dropping a few inches down his flies. A Union flag and rampant lion were tattooed on one bare arm, the other had a galleon with cannons blasting, a St George flag on its main mast.

Bessie was cooking a fry up in their tiny kitchen. The sausages and onions were turning his stomach over, his tongue welling saliva.

'How much longer?' he yelled.

'Nearly ready,' called Bessie from the kitchen.

'Nearly bloody doomsday.' Under his T-shirt, he scratched his belly button which was itchy with sweat. 'I phoned. I expect it on the table when I get in. You've nothing else on but a few errands for that geriatric busybody. Move it! Or get me belt.'

He'd come back early. Hardly any work on. He needed another firm, with all the Pakis taking over. His office had taken on half a dozen, most of them could hardly speak English – and now, just as he'd said, there wasn't enough work to go round.

They buckle down, his boss insisted. Do unsocial hours without argument. The English are lazy. That got Frank so angry, he couldn't speak. If he had've done so he'd have been sacked on the spot. Niggers, Pakis, Poles taking work away from the English workman. Whose country is it? Who fought in the war? His family. All these bleeding liberals, opening the gates wide. Come in! Come in! Here's family credit – have lots of kids. Need a Council flat? Jump the queue, my brown skinned friend. AIDS, TB – the NHS is all yours, please have a bed.

Whose country? The question was an obsession. With only one answer. But it was being stolen as he watched. Paki shops opening all hours, Poles, Russians, Turkish, taking over the high street. Women in black robes with slits for eyes crowding the supermarkets. It made him furious, the tearing away of his birthright. Just look at Green Street, round the corner, a total Paki takeover, hordes of 'em shopping and just up from the Hammers ground n'all. All over the town they were. He saw them in his cab, where he had to be polite, yes sir, no sir, what's the address of your drug dealer? And here, when he came home to what should be his castle, right here in this house, a mongrel couple breeding. A half caste growing in her belly.

Bessie brought him out his plate and put it on the table on a place mat. Two sausages, bacon, two eggs and fried bread. She went back out again and brought in the bread and butter. Out again for the sauce and mustard. And then out once more to bring her own in.

'I've put the kettle on for another cuppa,' she said.

'Is that all you're having?' he said, now at the table, indicating her single sausage and egg.

'Plenty for me,' she said, sitting down opposite. 'How's your day been?'

'Not enough work, too many Paki drivers,' he said, mouth full of sausage, yellow teeth and gaps to match his daughter's.

His hair was greying and receding quickly. He combed it forward in an attempt to fool the world that he had more than he had. He was clean shaven, shaving twice a day. Beards were intellectual, liberal, like sandals and muesli, anti-English.

She said cautiously, 'Are we going to the meeting this evening?'

'In the mongrels' flat?'

She nodded, knowing who he meant, correct or not.

'I've been thinking about it,' he said, as he dipped fried bread in egg. 'Have some bread.'

'I'm not very hungry.'

'Have some or get a slap.'

Bessie rapidly took a slice and bit into it to show willingness.

'It's a lot of money. Too much,' he went on with his former thread, 'but do we want to go into their flat? She's white for God's sake!' He thumped the table. 'White men not good enough for her?'

'So we're not going then?' she said carefully, taking a dainty bit of sausage and remembering a bite of bread.

'I want to know what their flat looks like.' He smiled at her. 'Know your enemy and all that. And I don't want to pay all that out.' But the economics didn't hold him long. 'She's a good looking woman. A teacher – for God's sake. I can't make it out, with that nignog.'

'Some teachers...,' said Bessie, not sure what she was going to say or what she meant, but feeling the necessity to agree with him.

'He comes out in the morning, wearing a suit. Just down from the trees. And has the cheek to wear a tie. It makes me laugh when I don't want to cry.' He took a slice of buttered bread and through a mouthful added, 'But we're going. It's good manners, and neighbourliness to our mongrel pair.'

'Mrs Home and Anne will be there.'

'So they will,' he said. 'White backup.' He wiped the egg on his plate with the slice. 'One of our lot should have called the meeting. Strategic mistake. But let's make the best of it and case the enemy's joint. You never know.'

And he smiled to himself as he chewed the last bit of bacon. Yes, Anne would be there. He knew that for certain as he'd met her first thing that morning, when he was going out for work and she was putting her rubbish in the bins.

They'd discussed the maintenance charge and the meeting. She said she was going, and on the spot he'd decided he was too. Ample flesh in the right places, he'd like to get some of that. White of course.

He was light and charming to her, or so he thought, agreeing that the charge was too much and it wasn't right, and something should be done. And they, as neighbours, should support each other.

Chapter 5

Jack returned with the empty wheelbarrow. The fallen chunk of the wall had gone into the skip. Heavy work, sledgehammering and chucking the bricks into the barrow. Some club hammer and cold chisel work, but limited skill all in all, just graft, knock it down, take it away. Now the rest of the wall on either side of the gap was leaning twenty degrees or more. Big storm, and that could come down too. He wriggled his neck and shoulders, building up quite a sweat hammering and carting away, the goggles itchy.

He needed to phone that girl. Get her to take her plants out in front of the first bit he was going to knock down. He regretted he'd promised her. It could be all hassle if she wasn't in. But he'd done it now.

The French windows opened and a tall, slim woman beckoned.

'Mr Builder, can I have a word?'

Nice looker, good figure. Yes, he'd give her a word gladly. About his own height, wearing green jeans and an orange T-shirt. She had a couple of toddlers behind her, one pulling at her legs. He crossed to her.

'Yes, madam. What can I do for you?'

She smiled at him, then broke off. 'Stop it, Dominic.'

'Lisa took my biscuit,' moaned the little one pulling her jeans.

'It was mine!' wailed the one behind.

She held up a hand to Jack. 'Just let me sort these two out. Won't be a sec.'

And she went back in, ushering the two toddlers into the room. Jack might have followed if he wasn't covered in dust. Curious, he gazed into the room. Toys were lying about on a PVC tiled floor, made up of red, white and blue squares. There was a rocking horse and a playpen, and on the walls brightly coloured nursery rhyme posters with an assortment of people, children and animals gambolling cartoon style. The woman sat the two children in red toddler-size chairs by a toddler- size table with milk and biscuits. And then came back out.

'They yours?' he said.

She shook her head vehemently. 'No, they go home, thank goodness. I'm a childminder.' She hesitated. 'I would offer you a cup of tea, but it's difficult at the moment...'

'Don't worry,' he said. 'I've a thermos. And I can see you've got your hands full.'

She smiled again. He liked her freckles, lightly sprinkled about her cheeks and forehead. Her hair was short with a slight fringe at the front. He was aware of staring, a little gormlessly, though she didn't seem to mind. He looked into her eyes, and felt a snatch of electricity. She didn't look away.

'Nice setup you've got there,' he said.

'It works,' she said, her eyes continuing to hold his.

Jack thought – is she playing, or what? He'd been caught out before, mistaking a little flirting for something more.

She turned away and indicated the wall.

'I normally bring the children out into the garden to play. But I can't do that with you swinging a sledgehammer.'

'Sorry, Miss is it?'

She nodded. 'Miss. Anne.'

Good so far, single. He said, 'Jack. Best keep the kids in. All the dust and bricks, no good for little 'uns. I should be a couple of days knocking the wall down and carting it away. Then you can come out again while I put the new fence in. Sorry for the inconvenience.'

'It's not your fault, Jack.' And she touched him lightly on the arm. 'You've a job to do. And that wall is dangerous.'

Then she hesitated. 'Do you mind me asking you a personal question?'

He smiled. She'd used his name and touched him, and now a personal question.

'Depends what it is,' he said.

'We've a meeting this evening,' she said. 'We're all leaseholders. And the agents are charging us for your work... So I wondered, if you wouldn't mind saying, how much you were getting?'

'You think the agent might be overcharging?'

She nodded.

He hesitated, then what the hell – she wasn't a tax inspector.

'£970 and that includes materials,' he said. 'That's for knocking down the wall, getting it taken away in skips and putting in a fence. I know you've got another builder coming in. I don't know why two of us...'

'Because I complained about that wall,' she said. 'I told them it was a danger to my children. Said I'd call a solicitor if they left it in that condition.'

'That accounts for it,' said Jack. 'It was a last minute job. The other builder probably wasn't free. I was. And got this dog-end.'

'They're charging us two thousand each,' she said, her lips tight. 'Eight thousand in all.'

'I can only talk about what I'm contracted for,' he said. 'Not the total. So I can't tell you whether that's fair or not.'

'It never stops,' she said, suddenly blowing a squall. 'It cost me a fortune getting my flat up to standard for childminding – and now these bastards want another two thousand...'

There came a wail from inside, and then another.

She touched him on the arm again. 'Sorry, Jack. You don't want to hear my moans. I dare say you've got your own. I'll invite you in for a cuppa when I'm a bit freer.' And as she went inside she added, 'Nice to meet you.'

'And you too,' he called after her.

There was someone he'd like to have a cuppa with. And biscuits. A Miss, good sign. Own flat. But might there be a boyfriend? There usually was in his experience. Sort that out before going overboard.

Now he'd better phone that daffy girl.

Chapter 6

She leaned on the supermarket trolley, her stick and handbag inside. She was breathing heavily, her legs aching. These aisles at Morrison's were so long and they kept moving things. She was sure the soap powder was here last week. Now what had they done with it?

She rested against the trolley. No rush. Dial-A-Ride wouldn't be back for forty minutes. And the driver was often late with all the traffic around Stratford. Mostly she had quite a wait when she'd finished her shopping, not that she minded, she could watch all the comings and goings. And there was the tea shop. And they had a toilet here. She was always curious what people had in their trolleys. All that bottled water, big bottles of it. What was the tap for? And really, she wanted to say, don't buy your meat here, go to your local butcher. It's better and cheaper. When you get to my age you don't have the choice, but you youngsters do.

She hated the two for the price of ones. They were a swindle. She didn't want two, the second lot would only go off. So she felt ripped off if she bought just the one, but when you live on your own – you have to. They don't care, these supermarkets. Pretend they do. Valued customer and all that rubbish.

She'd read a dairy farmer's tale in one of her magazines, how the supermarkets paid them less than it cost farmers to produce the milk. Take it or leave it, was their motto. She'd pay a few coppers more if she knew it went to the farmers. Always bought free-range eggs; chickens should have ground to run and peck on. Her mum kept chickens during the war, had a little run in their backyard, half a dozen they had. She loved finding the new-laid eggs in the morning when Mum sent her out to feed the chickens. Though she was afraid of the cockerel. She kept back from him. Sometimes he'd stride right up to her. Shoo! shoo! she'd shout and wave – but he wouldn't go away.

Fancy remembering that.

Which cornflakes? All these fancy cereals. You'd never believe there could be so many. All stuffed with sugar. No wonder the kids were losing their teeth. Own brand was cheaper. Biscuits? Well, she did like one or two with her tea, and so did Bessie. Millie was coming tomorrow. She liked shortbread. Own brand? Go for the posh ones for Millie. She'd probably bring a cake. Usually a walnut cake. They'd only have a couple of slices, but she and Bessie could finish it.

Bessie was a nice girl. She should look after herself better. It was that father of hers she blamed, the bullying man.

And as if she'd called him up, like a sorceress, she saw him. There, in the biscuits and crisps aisle, was Bessie's father. She was sure of it. He hadn't seen her. If she could run, she'd hit him smack in his fat belly with her trolley, and say – that's for kicking Tickles.

She approached him. She would not let him get away with it. He was picking through custard creams, deciding how big and sugary he wanted the pack. Very, it seemed. Two big, cheap packs he was weighing up.

She couldn't wait for his coronary, and tapped him on the shoulder with her walking stick.

'I want an apology from you.'

He turned, startled. And grabbed the stick, pulling it off her.

'Oi – give me that back,' she declared.

'Like fuck I will.' He smirked at her and smacked his open hand with the stick.

'You kicked my cat deliberately,' she said, standing her ground.

'Was it yours?' he said nonchalantly.

'You know very well it was mine.'

'I thought it was a stray. And I thought a good kick and it won't come back.'

He was resting on her stick like a gent, teasing her. She shouldn't get angry, but he was such a rotter. And shouldn't be allowed to get away with it.

'It's not the first time,' she retorted. She wasn't absolutely sure, but suspected it. Her cat had come back bruised before.

'An animal needs to know who's the boss,' he said. 'Just like you do. You silly old cow.'

'How dare you, you rude, insolent man!'

She was making her way round the trolley to him, hand by hand. That pink, fat face needed a slap.

'Your cat's so fat, it can barely waddle,' he said. 'Never mind a kicking, a mercy killing. And you too, just taking up useful space. Your flat's full of rubbish, all to be taken to the tip when you're gone.'

She lifted a hand to smack him but he grabbed her wrist. And jerked her away from the trolley. He threw the stick in the cart and began wheeling it away. She tottered and grabbed at a shelf of biscuits, pulling at a cluster that fell, leaving her holding air and staggering. Completely unbalanced, she went down.

Frank, a few metres away, stopped and turned about, and grinned at his elderly neighbour. She was splayed out on the supermarket floor, surrounded by packets of garibaldi.

He rattled her trolley. 'You won't need this anymore.' He lifted a can out. 'Especially not the cat food. I'll put it back for you. Save your cash and starve the moggy.'

And he headed off with the trolley. She scrambled on the ground, crawling after him along the floor of the aisle, flapping like a seal that had just come out of the sea.

'Come back! Stop thief!'

He took no notice, and continued down the aisle. She

watched him helplessly. Then sat up and began to weep. She was just a stupid old woman. He was right. She had lived too long. The world took no notice of her. Oh, she wished she was with John in the grave reserved for her.

'Are you alright, Madam?'

A young woman put a hand on her shoulder. She had a shopping trolley with a child sitting and facing her. She bent down and helped Nancy to her feet. Nancy held her shoulder as she rose.

'Thank you, young lady. You're very kind.' She let go of her shoulder and held on to the trolley, catching her breath, burning off the humiliation. 'Oh, look at all those biscuits. I should put them back.'

They were scattered like logs from a fallen wood pile.

The young woman shook her head. 'Oh, don't worry, someone'll pick them up. You leave them.'

'My trolley's been stolen,' she said plaintively, catching the eye of this kind young woman.

'Is that it?' The young woman pointed down the aisle at an abandoned cart.

Nancy peered. 'I don't know. Could be.'

The young lady patted her on the hand. 'Probably is. I'll get it for you.'

'Oh, you are a dear. Thank you.'

She watched her walk down the row. Oh, she'd been stupid. Fancy taking on that bully. At her age, in her condition. What could she have done to him? But you can't just let him kick your cat and get away with it. Except sometimes you just have to. What a silly old woman she was!

She gazed at the child who was licking a lollipop.

'You think I'm a silly old woman too, don't you?'

The child held out the lollipop for her to lick. And she laughed.

'Everyone gets old, you know. When you're young you just don't believe it will ever happen. But it does. Look at me now. I was as young as your mother once. Believe that if you can.'

The young woman returned with the trolley. With her was a young black man in a dark brown suit with an official looking name-badge in his lapel.

'She's had a fall,' said the young woman indicating Nancy. 'I wonder if you'd be so kind as to help her.'

'Of course,' said the young man. 'I'll just put these biscuits back.' He turned to Nancy. 'And then help you with your shopping, madam.'

He smiled at her, and she regretted all her thoughts about supermarkets. And how they rip you off. Well, they still did. But there were kind people, even here.

And nasty ones too.

Chapter 7

Jack was in his van on Ham Park Road outside the semi-detached house. On the other side of the road were the railings of West Ham Park, shrubs and trees along the edge. A Muslim woman was coming along the pavement, pushing a child in a pushchair. She was in black down to her feet, just a narrow gap for her eyes. He'd almost grown accustomed to such women, they were common these days. He mustn't stare. He'd had too many arguments about what people believed and didn't. At Alcohol Halt, some real fundamentalists there. It didn't stop them being drunks.

And there, another woman with her skirt halfway up her thighs, heavily made up. She gave him a bright smile, thrusting out her chest. He waved her off and she grimaced. He wondered how many men she'd had today. And what he'd catch if he joined them. Maybe the burqa wasn't such a bad idea.

Lunch time, for saints and sinners. He took his phone out of the glove compartment. He'd left it there while he was swinging his sledgehammer, not wanting to risk damage. A self-employed builder needs a phone. A job might come up anytime. You always have to think where the next one is coming from.

He leaned back in the seat and wriggled his shoulders and neck. All that hammering and humping. He'd have a good soak tonight. The van window could do with a wash, so could the van for that matter. He switched on his phone. A missed call from Alison, his ex-wife. Best phone back or she'd only get shirty.

Let's hope she's not in a mood.

He picked her out from his contacts and rang.

'Hello, Jack.'

'You called?'

'Can you stop buying Mia Enid Blyton books?'

'She says she likes them.'

'She's outgrown them.'

'That's not what she says.'

'Then she should have outgrown them. Have you ever read Enid Blyton?'

'No.' Puzzling whether this was a deficiency in his education she was pointing out.

'Try one. And in the meantime look for something with better vocabulary and characterisation.'

'What can you expect from a Daily Mirror reader?'

She sighed. 'Not a lot. I learnt that to my cost. Can you look after her this evening?'

He thought for a second. It'd mean not going to Alcohol Halt, but that could get pretty tedious with competitive tales of how much I used to drink – what a rat I was to my family, but aren't I good now! Besides, he could go on Wednesday. The same recovering alkies would be there. He should keep it up.

'Yes, alright. Bring her over. Anything else?'

'I've got an interview for a job in Brighton. Deputy Head.'

That was a surprise. Just when he thought things had settled down.

'Mia won't like moving,' he said. 'Losing her friends.' And her dad, he thought but didn't say.

'She's already made that clear.'

'You won't be able to bring her over at the drop of a hat.'

'And she won't get any more Enid Blytons, and tell me what's in the Daily Mirror... In Brighton, she can become a solid Guardian reader.'

'Will she still want to talk to me?'

'I doubt it. One learns painfully. See you at six tonight.'

She rang off.

She always left him seething. The underlying criticism,

some petty point scoring. She was better at it than he was. Her university education or reading the Guardian or just knowing his weak points? Never catch her reading the Mirror, or even eating her fish and chips from it. Should he get the Guardian himself? Upgrade. No thanks. There was so much of it. The Mirror he could read in half an hour. He didn't want a book, just a quick comic.

He gathered up his lunch bag, his thermos, his Mirror, gave the latter a flick with his finger to confirm it as his chosen badge, and got out of his van. A little chilly still, but the wind had dropped. He'd eat in the park. He'd considered having his lunch in the garden where he was working but that girl had offered him another cup of tea, a third, and he didn't want to say no again. Or have her standing over him and chatting while he ate. And then all those windows, the prying eyes of the house and its neighbours, he felt utterly scrutinised. He had to get away for half an hour at least.

He'd taken off his overalls and given them a shake out to get rid of the brick dust. Half respectable. He'd have liked to wash his hands, but then he'd have had to ask someone, as he'd already done with that childminder to use her toilet. What was her name? Anne. Anyway, it was just sweat, as he'd been wearing gloves to protect his hands; it would add salt.

As he entered the park, the sun came out from the clouds. The light and warmth lifted him. Horse chestnut leaves lay like discarded gloves on the bitumen path. Those remaining were blotchy yellow and green, fluttering in the sunlit breeze. He picked up a conker; it was new out of the shell, shiny brown as if polished with beeswax. He put it in his pocket. Overnight it would lose the shine, but for now it was magic. He didn't want to go too far in. A short break, this would be. And seated himself on a bench about sixty yards from the entrance, just far enough to mute the traffic, the cricket pitch in front of him, the wickets cordoned off till play began again next May. A cuboid, noisy machine with a man inside was going up and down sucking in leaves.

He thought of going elsewhere to get some quiet, but it was too much trouble. He wouldn't be here long. To the side was the children's playground, quiet at midday.

A man in a turban was cycling through the park. That was against the by-laws, he knew, but there was no one to stop him. West Ham Park had been a regular park of Jack's ever since he was a youngster growing up in Plaistow. He'd come here with his school and learnt about its history. The park was owned by the Gurneys, rich Quakers, in the 19th century; their London estate. Elizabeth Fry lived here. Then it was sold to the City of London in Victorian times, and had been a park ever since. There was a house once, Upton House, knocked down just after the war. Once in a very dry summer he'd made out oblong markings in this very field which must have been outbuildings, stables and sheds probably. Then there was the time he and some other builders, working nearby, one lunchtime had put down their coats on the grass for a kickabout, and had been ordered off by the parkkeepers. It was in the by-laws, they said. Jack and his mates argued – what harm were they doing? And the parkkeepers threatened to bring the police. It was absurd. A kickabout! Why? He'd never trusted the City of London after that. All those bankers and Guilds making stupid rules in an East End park.

He came here with Mia sometimes. She wasn't too old for the playground, well sometimes she was and sometimes she wasn't. They'd come for a picnic on summer Sundays. It could get very crowded. Lots of people breaking the by-laws. So that was the way to do it, in numbers. Then no one got bothered by the City bankers.

On the seat he laid out his newspaper, lunch bag and thermos. Two cheese sandwiches and an apple, not a lot, but enough to keep him going. You could spend a fortune at lunchtime going in cafes. It mounted up over a week. He could save maybe twenty pounds by making his own lunch, and while it was still warm, it was pleasant to sit outside.

He was finishing the second cheese sandwich when he saw her enter the park. The two toddlers were on leads while the baby was in a pushchair. Quite an obstacle course, he thought, getting across the road with that trio.

As she approached, she waved to him.

He waved back.

She wore a light jacket, bright red, almost overpowering in its brightness. She was coming slowly, the two children tugging at different angles to be free, while she pushed the pushchair at a regular speed no matter what, the leaves catching in the wheels and swishing out. His blood fizzed. It wasn't fair, how he could be taken over like this. Eating his lunch, cursing at the City, and whoosh. Hormones.

She stopped when she got to him. The baby grinning, waving at him, the two toddlers backing into Anne shyly.

'Hello,' she said, 'we're just going to the playground.' She smiled brightly, her eyes widening. 'Do you want to come?'

'Aren't I a bit old for the seesaw?'

'These three are our entrance ticket.'

'Then I'll come.'

He grinned and rapidly packed his things. Such invitations didn't come often enough. And you never know.

'You're getting on well with that old wall,' she said.

'Sooner it's down the better. Tedious job, breaking it up and carting it away. Feels like the Great Wall of China, never ending. Any idiot could demolish it.'

'I'm sure you're not an idiot,' she said earnestly.

'My ex thinks I am. I read the wrong paper and give my daughter Enid Blyton books.'

'Famous Five or Secret Seven?' she said.

'Famous Five,' he said.

'There's only 21 of them. I read them all when I was 9 or 10, maybe three times. And then I'd had enough. Blyton phase done with, and then never read another one. Try the Narnia books or E Nesbit. I don't think your ex will complain about those.'

'You can be my literary consultant,' he said.

'Pleased to.' She mock bowed.

He accompanied her into the playground where they headed for the swings. There were only a few others there, mostly young children with their mothers, though there was an elderly Sikh pushing a boy on the roundabout.

They took over the baby swing section, which they had to themselves. The two toddlers were put in a swing and secured, and then the baby taken out of the pushchair and put in one too. Jack joined her pushing them, the baby hardly at all, just the slightest of arcs, but the twins enjoyed the to and fro of gravity's play.

'How did you get into childminding?' he said.

'Oh, I had some trouble with my ex. Hell more like. And came down south. And couldn't get a job. So after countless rejections, I decided to work for myself. And thought childminding can't be difficult... so I did some volunteer work in a nursery for a few months. Then had my place done up with some money I still had. Passed the inspection. And advertised. And here I am, six months later.'

'Do you like it?'

'Sometimes. Depends on the kids, depends on me. We have our moods.' She laughed. 'I have a routine. We come to the playground every day, weather permitting. We draw and paint, I read to them, sing even.' She flapped her hands and laughed at herself. 'They don't know what a bad voice I've got. They're very appreciative. It's the parents can be difficult. I need a regular income, and they keep changing the rules. And the trouble is I'm too soft. Then I lose money.'

'That's the problem of being self-employed,' he said. 'Getting paid.'

'I should have a fourth child,' she said ruefully, 'though three is a handful. I'll stick with that till I'm better at it. I'll tell you one thing though...' She sighed as she gave the baby a little push. 'I get desperate for grown up company. All day with toddlers and babyspeak – and I am dying for an adult conversation. Someone to listen to me. To say long words. If there's no one else, I go to the pictures. Twice a week sometimes. There's a confession.'

She turned to him. He was pushing the boy twin who protested at going too high, so it was a light role. It needed precision.

'Do you want to come for dinner this evening?' she said.

Almost overwhelmed by the offer, he couldn't hide his eagerness. 'Love to.' Then a second later, with a sag of frustration, he recalled his earlier booking. 'Can't. Sorry. I've got to look after my daughter this evening. Twenty minutes ago, I told her mum I would.'

Her face fell, though she worked to hide it. Could he get out of having Mia? Too much hassle, he had agreed to it.

'I'm free tomorrow,' he said hopefully.

She clapped her hands. 'That's fine. Let's do tomorrow,' she said. 'There's a leaseholders' meeting tonight, so dinner would've been late anyway.'

'What time?'

'Make it 7,' she said. 'Flowers'll be nice, a bottle of wine – or is that cheeky of me?'

He shifted in his collar. 'I don't drink,' he said. And took a deep breath, but it had to be said. 'I'm in recovery,' he added, feeling himself going bright red. It was like confessing to child abuse. 'I've been off the juice for over a year now. And it has to stay that way.'

'Thank you for telling me,' she said.

'You can drink if you want,' he said. 'It's just I can't.'

'No, no,' she said. 'I won't. So you won't be tempted.'

He wondered how she felt about that. If she regretted asking him. Well, he'd told her, and there was no way out of that.

'My life depends on me staying dry,' he said. He knew it was a desperate thing to say, too much at a first meeting, but it was true and better said than not. 'Drink kills everything.'

Visions of hangovers and vomit, waking up in strange places, rows with Alison, jobs lost...

'I'm sure we can have a great evening without booze,' she said.

He hoped she meant it. But there it was, out in the open. And had to be. Much better when you knew where you were, and there were no surprises.

She'd gone silent, and he wondered whether he'd been a bit heavy. But what do you do? Hide it? And then she pours two glasses and assumes... No. Alcohol Halt said there would always be surprises, but avoid whatever you can.

'Who else lives in the house?' he said, eager to get the subject off his weakness. 'I've met Bessie. She keeps making me tea. It's too weak for my liking, but she means well. And she has to come out all the time to move her plants in case I drop a brick on them.'

'Her dad bullies her,' said Anne. 'Frank. He keeps trying to chat me up. I have to be polite but he won't take a hint. I know we're going to end up enemies. Then there's Nancy, the old woman. She wants my flat, I can tell. I do feel sorry for her, all those stairs, but I need the ground floor for childminding. Then up top there's Maggie and David. She's a teacher, very nice, and David manages a coffee shop. Rather wrapped up in each other.'

'They must be in love.'

'They'll get over it.'

'So cynical, so young.'

She was pushing the swing, deliberately not looking at him. He wondered about her ex, about the hell. Keep it light, keep it frothy. He kicked some leaves. There was always hell.

'This used to be a big house for toffs once, the park,' he mused, 'The Gurneys...'

'Quakers,' she said. 'They didn't drink either. Porridge oats and chocolate.'

'I'll bring you a big box,' he said, and looked at his watch.

'Must get back. I hope my conversation has been adult enough.'

'Fair to middling,' she said with pressed lips. 'I will feel grown up till tea time. And thank you for pushing a swing.'

'Thank you for inviting me to dinner.'

He put a hand over hers as she held the chain of the swing. She gave a sharp intake of breath as if his fingers were hot but didn't pull her hand away.

A little damp hand came over theirs, a twin protesting at the slowing swing. They untwined, and grinned shyly at each other.

He began to back away. 'Someone has to knock that wall down.'

'Someone has to push the swings.' She blew him a kiss.

He didn't want to go, but didn't want to be seen as needy. Let it come at its own pace, if it came. Blundering in never works. He walked out of the playground, glancing back as he took the path to the Ham Park Road gate. She was busy with the threesome, singing them something, now that he was almost out of earshot.

Chapter 8

The rest of the afternoon he worked on the wall. His aim was to complete the half going to the back fence today. Get that all knocked down and taken out to the skip. The full skip was being taken away in the morning and an empty one dropped off. Tomorrow's plan was to knock down and cart away the other half, the length of brickwork going to the house. The weather was holding, but you never knew with outside jobs. Though it wasn't dangerous work, so he'd work on through rain unless it was a real thunderstorm.

Bessie had taken out all her plants as far as the fence. They lay in a line of soily roots and straggled leaves on the lawn, away from where Jack was working. He found he minded her less when she was busy, her chat perhaps a little inane but she was pleasant enough. He was impressed by her efficiency; once she realised what was needed, she was off. With a small handsaw and a pair of secateurs, she pruned the climbing rose hard back, and cut the ties that held it to the wall. He wondered why she was always at home. She wasn't stupid and could work hard enough. From what she said he felt it had something to do with her father who drove a cab. He was curious about their relationship but didn't pry; he had work to do and his own life to dwell on.

From time to time he glanced at the French windows, and occasionally caught a glimpse of Anne, and more occasionally caught her looking out at him, when both would give a wave of recognition, like two goldfish trapped in their respective bowls.

The sun had gone in, but Jack although in a T-shirt had built up enough heat to not care. He looked up at the clouds, he'd become quite a weather watcher and knew the clouds to watch out for. These were patchy stratocumulus and layered in some places, but had plenty of blue spaces. It was once the blue was shut out that rain might follow.

He wanted to go out with his telescope tonight. His daughter Mia knew her craters of the moon. It was a favourite for the two of them. There was a half moon tonight, better for viewing than a full moon. The sky was probably clear enough, and might improve. He thought about the possibility of her going to Brighton. And didn't like it. Well, Alison would have to get the job first. Worry about that one when it's real.

Late afternoon, he accepted an offer of a cup of tea from the girl. Sweaty and dusty; it was good to get the gloves and goggles off for ten minutes. And have a stretch. The girl didn't have her tea with him but had brought down an old, rusting, oblong biscuit box, along with his tea. She was gathering up bits and pieces from the garden and putting them in. A slug, was that? He couldn't help his curiosity.

'What are you doing?'

'Magic,' she said. She spoke to him confidently now. He'd been kind to her, was protective as he could be of her plants and always thanked her for tea and biscuits.

'You a witch?' he said as he supped.

'I know a few spells,' she said cautiously.

Her tone made him realise she took this seriously. But he didn't.

'Can you magic me up the name of the Derby winner?'

She shook her head, and screwed up her face at his lightness.

'I don't know any white magic,' she said. 'Only black.'

She was examining a piece of muddy root, rejected it and tossed it aside.

'What magic have you done?' he said.

She was crouching on the ground, looked up at him and bit her lip.

'I can't tell you,' she said at last.

Jack finished the last of his tea. He didn't believe in witchcraft but the girl plainly did. He shouldn't be so dismissive – but couldn't help it.

'Are you wicked?' he said.

She chewed her thumb. 'Not mostly,' she said, 'only when I'm forced to be.'

He stared at her, her very white skin and blue eyes. She wasn't kidding.

'Promise you won't change me into a frog.'

She half shrugged and grinned. 'I can't do that.'

'What can you do?'

She closed her box and stood up.

'Not telling you.'

And clutching her box close to, she ran across the grass into the house.

He watched her disappear in the back door. Bet next week's wages she was going to put a hex on someone. Would she do it on Alison for him? Change her into a snake. He grinned at his meanness, his stupidity. Amazing people still believed in that medieval stuff. It reminded him of the woman in the burqa. You don't have to look hard to find the primitive in all communities. But Bessie specialised in black magic. Pins in dolls, he imagined, but what about love potions? Which made him glance at the French windows. Anne wasn't in sight but he could see one of the twins on a rocking horse. Tomorrow, dinner. Then what? He couldn't help fantasising. Bed perhaps. Knew it never paid to think too far ahead. Sure he wanted sex, but didn't want to be ensnared in some sticky relationship. Anne had said something about the hell of her ex. What was that about? Serious enough for her to run away from it.

He put his goggles back on and then his gloves. He picked up the sledgehammer and stepped through the gap into next door's garden. Swinging back the sledgehammer he took aim at a section of wall, and heaved at it. The head struck with a bouncing thump and the mortar shivered and cracked. Another whack, and a clump of half a dozen bricks fell to the earth.

Chapter 9

Nancy was seated in her armchair, her feet on a pouffe. The gas fire was on, the window closed. Bessie at the table found it rather stuffy in the room but didn't complain. It wasn't her flat and she knew Nancy needed it warm. The old lady was watching her as she took bits and pieces out of the old biscuit tin and laid them on the table.

'Have you got everything?' said Nancy.

'Yes, everything,' said Bessie without looking up. 'Come to the table, please.'

She was arranging the objects in the shape of a pentagon. A buttered penny one corner, an oak gall the second, a forked root another, a worm stuck through with a pin the fourth, a pinned slug the last.

Nancy took her feet off the pouffe and, pushing on the seat arms, stood up. Gripping one of the table chairs, she took the few steps to the sitting room table. And then sat herself down, opposite Bessie. She grimaced at the worm and slug, the former wriggling helplessly on its pin.

'I hope you are going to clean up afterwards, Bessie.'

'Of course,' said Bessie. 'Black magic is always messy. This one isn't so bad. One spell I used had an ox tongue and half a frog.'

'What happened to the other half of the frog?'

Bessie said she didn't know, but she did. She'd given it to Tickles, who was now licking himself on the rug in front of the gas fire.

'You know, I can't get over how he just pushed me over and stole my shopping trolley,' said Nancy. She rubbed her ribs which still ached.

'He does worse than that,' said Bessie, not quite happy

with the way the forked root was orientated.

'I was lucky that young woman helped me and got the manager... Morrison's, Stratford. He just left me lying on the floor and walked away laughing.'

Bessie switched the positions of the buttered penny and the oak gall.

'That will do,' she said. 'Now we have to put both our hands in the pentagon.'

Nancy put her hands in. Bessie adjusted them slightly and put hers over them.

'And now you must repeat after me, line by line.' She was looking at a rough piece of paper on which she'd copied out the spell. She began:

By this oak gall, I give you pain.
By this worm, I put hell in your brain.
By this slug, your bowels will shake.
By this buttered penny, your bones will break.
By this crooked root, I split you in twain.

At the end of the declamation, they stopped. A long pause for the magic to soak in.

'Please remove your hand,' said Bessie.

Both took their hands out of the pentagon. The worm still wriggled and the slug's back was arching against the pin.

'I have to put them away in exactly the right order,' she said. 'Oak gall, worm, slug, buttered penny and crooked root.'

One by one, they went in the tin. The pentagon had gone, the corners in the old biscuit tin.

'Now we have to decide what we want done to him.' She gave Nancy a small piece of paper and a pencil. 'Write on it in capital letters. Screw it up, don't let me see it, and put it in the tin.'

'Anything?' said Nancy.

'Anything you want done to him. In no more than three words.'

Nancy shivered and closed her eyes for an instant. Then wrote, her arm round it, like a schoolchild hiding her work. When done, she screwed up the paper and put it in the box. Her hand hesitated above the box as if she wanted to take it out again. But she left it there.

Bessie thought for a few seconds, her teeth gritted. Then wrote – DROP DOWN DEAD. She folded the paper in half and then screwed it up and put it in the box. She put the lid on and pushed it down hard.

She said, 'This must go under his bed tonight. And be left there all night, so the magic seeps into him as he sleeps. Then tomorrow night, when the moon is up, we must bury the box in the garden.'

Chapter 10

Maggie got to the front door just as Frank was opening it to go in. She'd thought of dawdling when she'd got out of her car and spotted him ahead of her going through the gate, but by then he'd seen her. So she smiled and waved as if she meant it. She might not love her neighbour but it made life easier to pretend friendliness.

He was shorter than her by a few inches, tubby, terrible teeth. Well, appearances were one thing and she'd learnt as a teacher not to judge by them. But there was a meanness about Mr Brand, a misanthropy. No, let's not disguise it, he was a wicked racist.

She could feel it by the way he was looking at her belly. She was six months pregnant and definitely showing. He twisted his lips – and was that a hiss?

Oh for heaven's sake, she was barely home and she'd had a bad enough day without dealing with this creep. She put down her shopping bag while he opened the door. She had marking in her backpack.

'Good afternoon, Mr Brand,' she said, giving him the best smile she could manage.

'Afternoon,' he said grudgingly, watching her belly all the time as if he would like to cauterise the contents.

'I do like a bit of Indian summer,' she said.

'Leaves are a nuisance,' he said.

What on earth could she reply to that?

'*Season of mists and mellow fruitfulness, Close bosom-friend of the maturing sun,*' she gathered up from a dusty attic area of her brain.

'What?' He looked up from her belly, puzzled.

'Autumn by John Keats,' she said. 'David and I like

autumn walks. The berries and the leaves turning.'

She knew it was a challenge mentioning her husband. But he did exist.

'How's your daughter?' she said to his silence.

'Fine,' he said, to cut that topic short, holding the door open for her.

With relief, she went in ahead of him. Though she felt uncomfortable with him walking behind her as she went through the hallway. She stopped for an instant to look at the post on the shelf, putting down the shopping, and let him get ahead. Now he wouldn't be examining her bum and legs in that foul head of his. His daughter though wasn't unpleasant, a little subdued; she could do with taking in hand clothes-wise and her teeth, but she was surprisingly nice considering the loins she'd come from.

There were a couple of letters. One a bill from the electric company, the other from Nigeria for David.

Frank was well up the stairs by the time she made her way up, keeping it purposely slow, as if it was her pregnancy. But it wasn't. She didn't want another encounter as she passed his door, and made sure he was inside. One was more than enough for the day.

Though there would be another with the meeting. She dismissed the thought, a couple of hours yet. And the others would be there. In fact, why not check on Nancy? See if she was alright and coming this evening. On the first floor landing, she rapped on her door.

'Nancy,' she called. 'It's me, Maggie.'

'Won't be a minute, dear,' came a call from inside.

Maggie felt she should keep an eye on the old lady, knowing she didn't have many visitors and a five minute chat was hardly out of her way.

Nancy came to the door, her hand on her stick, a little breathless. She gave a bright smile.

'Would you like to come in for a cuppa, dear?'

'I'll come in for a minute, no cuppa though. I've got to

get ready for this evening's meeting.'

She followed Nancy into her room, leaving her shopping by the door. So hot and stuffy. If it was hers she'd open a window immediately. Still, when she got to 87 who knows what temperature she'd want her sitting room?

Nancy sank heavily into her chair. Maggie felt she could hear the creaking of her bones as the old lady relaxed into the cushions.

'You should get a zimmer frame,' said Maggie. 'My granny has one. Makes life a lot easier round the house.'

'I should, shouldn't I?' said Nancy. 'My friend Millie says so too.'

'Why don't I take you to the doctor's during the school holidays and arrange it. It's only a couple of weeks from now.'

'Oh that's very kind of you, dear.' She smiled wearily. 'Sit down please, are you sure I can't make you a cup of tea?'

'No, Nancy, I just popped in to make sure you were OK.'

'I am now, but what a day I've had! I had a fall in Morrison's supermarket. Nothing serious.' She decided not to mention Frank's part in it. 'But it does throw you. They were very nice about it. The manager helped me with my shopping, and there was this young woman who got me to my feet...' She didn't care to mention the black magic which seemed rather silly to her now with its forked roots and slugs.

'Are you alright for the meeting this evening?' said Maggie.

'I'll be fine.'

'It might have been better to have had it here, instead of making you come up another two flights...' she stopped. 'Too late for that. There'll be a nice bit of cake for you. Marks and Spencer's coffee cake and some chocolate biscuits too. I'll come down and help you up the stairs.'

'No, dear, you have enough to do. I'll make my way up slowly.'

'I'll come down for you and that's that.' She rose. 'Do excuse me, Nancy, but I've quite a bit to do before the meeting. We need to get together every so often or the agent will just push us around.' She saw Nancy was about to rise. 'No, you stay there. I'll see myself out. And I'll come down about twenty past seven for you.'

Maggie went to the door where she gathered up her shopping bag, opened up and waved as she left.

'See you later.'

'Bye, dear.'

And closed the door.

Ooh, the heat of that room. Not that it helped her being in her outside clothes. But what must her bills be like! Sixty years to worry about that, if she ever made it. What with climate change and the bomb, might anybody? She continued up the stairs, past Frank and Bessie's flat where she could hear the TV droning. She gave the door two fingers. And climbed the final set of stairs to her own flat at the top of the building.

They'd have to leave the pram downstairs in the hall. Couldn't take it up and down three flights. Not that they wanted to stay here, but what you want and what you can afford don't always coincide.

She opened the door and let herself in. And with relief put down her shopping and took off her backpack.

By the time David was home, she'd put everything away and showered.

'Coffee, love?'

'Yes, please.' He pecked her on the cheek. 'Ooh, you smell nice.'

'Just for you, honey. And we have the meeting tonight. Remember? Meet the neighbours.'

David sank into an armchair. He was a slim, tall black man, about her age, mid 20s, smart in his dark blue suit and tie.

'I've been offered promotion,' he said with a proud smirk.

'What as?'

'Area manager.'

'What's the catch?' she said as she poured out his coffee.

'You might never see me.'

'Is that a catch?'

She put the coffee on the table beside him and went to kiss him on the forehead, and stumbled.

'Careful, careful, with the bump,' exclaimed David.

'So am I now just a vessel for your offspring?'

'A very lovely vessel.'

She sat on his lap. He put a hand on her tummy.

'I can feel him kicking,' he said. 'He doesn't want me to be area manager.' He held his hand firm against her belly. 'Listen, kid. My kingdom will stretch from Ilford out to Romford.'

'How do you feel about it, David?'

He sighed, taking his hand away. 'It was never my dream. I wanted to be a human rights lawyer, but I couldn't get a bloody job. So I took a temporary job in a coffee shop...'

'And in no time you were manager.'

'Then I met this high flying teacher...'

'Thank you very much.'

'And got her pregnant. And here we are stuck in a one-bedroom flat.'

She sat up. 'It does make things tricky. Do I go back to work or not? What's area manager worth?'

'Another seven thou a year.'

She sniffed. 'Well that's alright. But not enough if we want to buy our own place.'

'But that means the two of us working,' he sighed. 'And me never getting back to law.'

'Oh fuck it. I can't stand capitalism. It makes us all wage slaves, spending our lives grubbing away to buy houses which are way too expensive, simply to pay for our last years in care homes.'

'Beautiful analysis, dear. But no help. So if you'll kindly get off my lap...'

'Don't want to get off.'

She kissed him on the lips. He held her to him, and they murmured in mutual comfort for a minute.

She broke away.

'We've got guests in forty minutes.'

'Off, off, off.' He lifted her off and rose.

'How brutal you are.'

'I want a shower, change, need a bite to eat...'

'You shower. I'll make us scrambled egg on toast.'

'Go to it.'

And he strode off to the bedroom.

'Hey!' She picked up his coffee and took it after him.

Chapter 11

Alison was at his door with Mia, frowning. It was still light though the sun was low. The street trees had most of their leaves. He wondered what he'd ever seen in her. Objectively she was quite good looking, light make-up and shoulder length chestnut hair, her figure was holding out – but it was her tongue that wiped all that away. He didn't exactly want to kill her, but might be busy tying his shoelaces when the hitman took aim.

'Parking on this road is a nightmare,' she said. 'We had to wait for someone to leave. I don't know how you stand it.'

'Too many cars,' he said, indicating the lines on both sides of the road.

'And all the traffic in Homerton. At least the Olympic Park was pretty free. And then your high street...'

'It isn't mine,' he said. 'I don't own Forest Gate.' He opened the door wider. There was no point standing out here.

'I'm not coming in,' said Alison. Good, he thought. Keep it short and leave us in peace. She turned to Mia. 'Bed by eight thirty,' she said.

'That's far too early,' complained Mia. 'My friends stay up to ten and ten thirty even...'

'I'm not their mother,' said Alison, 'but I am yours. Eight thirty. And don't forget your homework.'

'I won't,' mewled Mia.

'Make sure she does it,' said Alison to Jack.

Jack nodded. He nodded to everything, it was quicker that way.

'I'll get her to school at 8.45,' he said.

'And make sure she washes properly.'

Mia scowled. Her intimacies discussed between her parents was one of the indignities of her childhood.

'And no more than half an hour on the internet.'

Jack nodded. He was weary of the list and just hoped she'd go, wherever she was going. A date maybe. He pitied the poor sod, the puritan mother and senior teacher would come out in the end, no matter what initial self she played out over dinner or wherever. Or was it just him? Objectivity was well out of the window and on its way to Spain. But she did look like she was going out. He couldn't damn her for that, but did anyway.

'When will you learn about Brighton?' he said.

'In the next day or two. If I get it, I shall have to work the term out here and start there next term.'

'Big change.'

She smiled brightly. Yes, she was attractive. All that energy and fire. He remembered it in their early days. Too bad he was a Mirror reader.

'Can we go in, Dad? I'm getting cold.'

'Anything else?' he said, hoping they could get it over without spitting in each other's eyes.

'What's that in your hair?'

He put his hand in his hair and looked at his fingers. 'Brick dust.'

'At least it means you're working, even if your personal habits leave something to be desired.'

'Leave it out, Alison. I've only been home fifteen minutes.'

'Your washing habits were one of the reasons...'

He cut her short. 'I assume that's everything, apart from my need for a shower which I will have as soon as I close the door on this lecture.'

Alison pressed her lips tightly together and turned on her heels. Smart, high heels. It was a date.

'I'll see you after school tomorrow, Mia,' and she was clipping down the path.

Jack closed the door on her retreating form. She exhausted him. A couple of minutes at the door, that was all it took. What was the point of it? They weren't going to get remarried. Yes, he'd been a bastard, a drunken bastard, he couldn't wriggle out of that one, so maybe he deserved what he was getting – but what was the point?

It might be better if she did go to Brighton. Except Mia would go with her.

Once upstairs in the flat, he said, 'We've a tight schedule. I'm going to have a shower, you are going to do your homework...'

'Oh Dad!'

'Because we are going out with the telescope to look at the moon, we'll grab a pizza to eat in the van...'

'Oh great! Where's the moon book?'

'Homework first. Let's get on the move – or it won't happen.'

Mia was rapidly unpacking her schoolbag.

Chapter 12

In the end David collected Nancy, while Maggie prepared the tea and coffee. This was all set out on the dining table with the cake, sliced into a slab each, and the biscuits laid out on a large plate, with a stack of small plates beside. She was the hostess, and wanted everything to go well. It was much better to get on with your neighbours. They helped you, you helped them. Just a little effort paid dividends over the years.

She'd taken one of the table chairs for herself. There had been some protest, but she'd proclaimed that pregnancy wasn't an illness, she was just a bit heavier. Nancy had been given an armchair, with extra cushion support. On the long sofa were Anne, Frank and Bessie. She had noted that Anne had tried to head off sitting next to Frank but it was unavoidable as plainly he wanted to sit next to her, and Bessie was pliable.

Nasty man, but if you were going to have a management meeting then you had to invite everyone, love them or loathe them. Besides, all their enmity could be directed at the agents for overcharging. A common enemy, that's what you needed for togetherness. She did so want the evening to go right. Just like her mother, she couldn't help it. When you invite people into your house, you are welcoming and hospitable. You want to be liked, for everyone to thank you for a nice time. It was your duty to offer every amenity to the guests in your tent, as primitive as Abraham.

David had the other armchair, but was helping her dish out the cake, coffee and teas. He gripped her hand over the table supportively. She nodded and winked. So far, so good. The cake was a winner. Expensive, but what the hell.

'This is a lovely room,' said Anne. Her coffee was on the long, glass-topped table in front of her, coffee cake on a plate with a pastry fork on her knee.

'Thank you,' said David. 'We decorated it together.' He leaned against his wife. 'Maggie chose the colour scheme.'

'I like the pictures,' said Bessie.

'Thank you,' said Maggie, smiling at her. 'They're prints I bought at the British Museum and had framed. I do like history.'

'Is that your family, David?' said Anne, indicating the group of black people in a photo on the sideboard.

'It's my cousins in Lagos,' he said. 'I haven't seen them for a couple of years. We should go over again. The flights are expensive but they put us up, so not a lot else to pay.'

'Except the presents for everyone,' exclaimed Maggie. 'That is so exhausting, so expensive...'

'It's the done thing,' excused David, 'if you only go every few years, you have to go laden with gifts. And then you are stuck, because they expect it next time.'

Maggie sat down and took a sip of coffee. David leaned forward in his armchair and began on the cake. The chow before the pow-wow.

'Let's have the baby first,' she said, nodding at David, 'before we plan another trip.'

'How many months is it now?' asked Anne.

Maggie caressed her protuberance. 'Six. There's someone awfully big in here.'

She saw Frank shuffling awkwardly. But really, it was obvious enough she was pregnant, and she should be able to discuss her own baby in her own home, for heaven's sake.

'Do you know the sex yet?' said Anne.

'It's a boy or girl,' laughed David. 'All this boy stuff in my culture is so primitive. It will be what it is – and will be loved, whatever.'

'Hear, hear,' added Maggie.

They needed to start the business, she thought. Quickly. Frank looked as if he was about to explode. His face was reddening, he was clenching and unclenching his fists.

'Well, all I can say,' said Anne, 'you are looking very well.' And added with a laugh, 'All three of you.'

'Do you think it's right...?' began Frank.

And she knew this was it. Knew it was all a mistake. Marks and Spencer's cake or not.

'...bringing a half-caste child into the world?'

'The term is mixed race, Mr Brand,' Maggie said icily.

'Politically correct nonsense,' he retorted. 'It'll be half and half. Neither one thing or the other. What sort of start in life is that?'

'A baby doesn't know anything,' said David.

'But his parents do.'

'Do you think I should have an abortion, Mr Brand?'

'In my humble opinion, yes. I do. Clean yourself out. Rid the world of a problem.'

David stood up, a vein heaving in his temple.

'I'd like you to leave this flat right now, Mr Brand.'

'I'm here for the meeting. This is a leaseholders' get-together to discuss the costs of the building work...'

'You have insulted me and my wife. Please leave.'

'I think it best you leave, Mr Brand,' said Maggie coldly.

It was too late, all over, nothing could be unsaid. All she believed about the man was true. She'd known it. Simply hoped he could be polite for once.

The evening was in ruins.

But Frank had not moved. He held his seat on the sofa. Bessie, beside him, was trembling.

'You're not having a management meeting without me,' said Frank. 'Agreeing things behind my back. Oh no. I knew it was a mistake coming here.' He looked around to Anne and Nancy for their agreement. 'One of us should have organised this meeting, not this mongrel couple...'

David swung a punch at Frank. It missed, but Frank half

rose and butted David in the stomach. David doubled over groaning. Maggie grasped Frank by his hair.

'You swine, you utter swine...' she yelled.

The coffee table tipped, spilling the china, toppling cake onto the carpet.

'You fucking, nigger loving cow!' screamed Frank, as she yanked his hair, jerking him over the fallen table, his arms flailing, trying to land a blow.

Frank kicked Maggie in the stomach. She gasped, collapsed, let go of his hair, and sank slowly onto the carpet like a holed ocean liner. David was on Frank, seated on his chest, pressing him to the ground and smashing him in the face. The cab driver's nose was bleeding, a tooth bent...

'Please, please, David. Stop.' Anne was pulling at his shoulders from behind. She was pale and distressed.

Maggie was groaning on the carpet. David stood up, looking down at his victim, his smeared fist ready for more.

'Get the fuck out! Now!'

Frank's face was a mess, blood dripping from a nostril, blood in an eye, a tooth hanging... He was snorting like a horse. He slowly rose from the carpet, crushed cake sticking to his trousers, keeping out of the way of David's fists.

'You'll be sorry for this, you black cunt.'

He grabbed Bessie by the arm. 'Let's get out of this brothel.'

His daughter was shivering as if she'd been sitting on ice, she looked about her wildly. Her father pulled her by the arm and dragged her out of the room. David slammed the door behind them. And pressed his back against it as if they might try to come back in. Then went to Maggie who was sitting up on the carpet looking round at the devastation.

'What a waste of fucking cake!'

Chapter 13

Nancy's heart was thundering, her breathing in short gasps. It had happened so quickly. So out of control, like a bolting horse. Frank got nastier and nastier. David asked him to leave and when he wouldn't go hit him, and then tables were flying, china hitting the floor. All she could do was pull up her legs and protect her face.

So quickly. The fight, what was it – a minute? Like a bomb going off – and here they were sitting in the debris counting corpses.

Anne was gathering up broken china and putting it in a black plastic bag. She would have helped herself but couldn't get down to the floor. Maggie, in spite of being six months pregnant, was collecting up any unbroken crockery. David was on his knees with the brush and pan, brushing up the cake and china fragments. She watched uselessly from her armchair, a hand to her pounding chest.

'That certainly went with a swing,' said Maggie.

'Fuck off, Maggie,' said David.

'I'm not getting at you, sweetie. You were wonderful,' she said, ruffling his hair. 'I'm glad you defended my honour.'

'And my own,' said David.

'Let's say family honour.' She put her load of china on the table. 'The bastard comes into our flat,' she went on, 'eats our cake, especially bought at huge expense from Marks and Spencer's, drinks our freshly ground coffee... And then suggests I should have an abortion because our child will be mixed race.' She laughs. 'Did his mother never teach him manners?'

Anne on her knees, broken china in both hands, stopped for a second, looking lost in the wreckage like a child, the sole survivor of a car crash.

'I am so sorry, Maggie, David. It was a shameful display. Such an abuse of your hospitality.'

She struggled to say more, gasping for words, for sense.

'It's his daughter I feel sorry for,' said David, sweeping half-eaten bits of expensive cake into his pan. 'The way he pushed her out. You wonder what he's doing to her now.'

'Poor girl,' said Nancy, shaking her head. 'She helps me a lot. Does my errands, helps me with Tickles... Her father is a monster.'

She recalled those minutes in the supermarket when he taunted her, stole her trolley and left her helpless on the ground. Her neck burned with embarrassment at her helplessness then and now, the awfulness of old age – everyone clearing up except herself.

'I'm sorry I can't help,' she began, 'but...'

'Stay there, Nancy,' said Maggie. 'We know your heart's in the right place.'

'There's plenty of us to clear up,' said David. 'Anyway, I broke the damn stuff...'

'All my beautiful cake,' said Maggie in a mock moan.

Before Nancy had met the upstairs couple she wouldn't have approved of, what did they call it? mixed race children, mustn't say half-caste, but they had both been so nice to her. Maggie dropping in to see her most days, David coming down this evening to help her up the stairs. Why would their child be a problem, except for people like Frank, and perhaps herself, she thought guiltily. She must take care with what she said. Just a word out of place and everyone is so offended. It's a different age.

Good luck to them.

Anne was on her haunches, her face red, as if she'd been working all night. She always said hello and how are you when they met in the hallway. And only last week had invited her in her flat with Tickles, and the children stroked him. Though Nancy couldn't say she knew her, not like

David and Maggie who were much more open. Who had organised the meeting, which should have been a lovely get together as well as being for business.

And Bessie was a lovely girl. Shame.

'You wonder why he came at all,' said Anne.

'Because he wouldn't be left out,' said David.

'I could see it building up in him,' said Maggie. 'I thought if we don't get on to business very soon... And then it was too late. He couldn't hold it in, his hatred of me and David. We have betrayed the white race.'

'I am so sorry,' said Anne. 'I mustn't keep saying that. But I am. What he's done to you and David. What he's done to the whole house. One man. All that destructive energy. I feel ashamed. It's why I keep apologising. I'm white too. He makes me ashamed of all of us.'

David put a hand on her shoulder.

'Don't be,' he said.

'You can't be responsible for that pig,' said Maggie. She dropped onto a dining chair, still holding a couple of cups. 'It's my husband I'm worried about. Such a peaceful chap, I thought when I married him. He's been offered promotion as area manager because he keeps such a cool head in a crisis.'

'They might well reconsider,' he said with a wry smile, 'if they'd seen Godzilla running amok tonight.'

'But really,' said Maggie, 'you had no choice. He wouldn't leave. You made it clear he'd gone beyond the pale with his insults. Any normal person would have known they were no longer welcome. But he sits tight, and, as if he hasn't said enough, piles on the offence.'

'I was afraid when he kicked you,' said Anne. 'For the baby.'

'Oh, that was terrible,' added Nancy. 'What sort of man does that?'

'Fortunately there's a water bag in there,' said Maggie. 'But didn't it hurt. Like being hit by a football.' She rubbed her tummy as she recalled the blow. 'They talk about the pre-natal effect. Could the baby hear the insults?'

'No,' said David. 'He only understands Yoruba.'

'Bollocks,' said Maggie. 'Excuse me, everyone, I don't normally swear. I am a teacher and can normally cope when all hell breaks loose. But this evening, I simply hoped a bit of hospitality, neighbourliness and cake would bring us together... The whole house, all four flats, a little bit of friendship and coffee cake.' She sniffed and her eyes filled with tears. 'For the first time in six months, I am thinking, just like that monster man – what world am I bringing my child into?'

David put his arm round her and led her to an armchair. She sat down, he on the arm, and she leaned against him.

'Sorry, Anne, Nancy.' She smiled weakly. 'These conflicting emotions, part of pregnancy I suppose, but I so wanted a pleasant little party.'

'Didn't we all,' said Anne.

'That'll do for the clearing up, Anne,' said David. 'Let's have a cup of tea. The British solution in a crisis. There's still some cake and all the biscuits. Don't let the bastard ruin our get together.'

David rose, heading for the kitchen.

'Can we have some music, dear?' said Maggie. David halted, considering what. 'Something soothing.'

'How about Beethoven's Pastoral?' he said, going to the music deck. 'The first movement,' turning to them with a grand gesture. 'The awakening of pleasant feelings upon arriving in the countryside.'

'Isn't he a wonderful manager?' exclaimed Maggie.

Chapter 14

Jack and Mia were on the top of the hill. The area virtually part of Epping Forest. Jack had searched for a place, not too far away, with clear, fairly unlit space around. And this was the best he could come up with. He could get here from Forest Gate in twenty five minutes if the traffic wasn't bad. There was a golf course to the south, farm land and forest in the other directions. It was roads and habitations you had to get away from if you wanted unpolluted skies. And this was half decent without heading out to the wilds of Dartmoor.

The sky had become clearer and a moon, just beyond half, was rising in the darkening twilight. Below, there was mostly fields and forest with the odd sprinkle of lights picking out roads and houses. Sparse. This was well-off Chingford, and if the houses were large, then so were their grounds. Jack and Mia were seated on a bench, the Newtonian telescope set up a couple of metres away, eating pizza and drinking tea from the thermos. They wore their observing gear: woolly hats and scarves, their fingerless gloves temporarily in the pockets of their jackets while they ate.

When they'd finished the pizza, they wiped their hands on a towel Jack had brought and put on their fingerless gloves. The rubbish went in the litter bin by the bench.

'Let's see what you can find on the moon,' said Jack as they went to the telescope. 'Keep close to the terminator for best viewing. How about Copernicus?'

'That's too easy, Dad.'

It pleased him that she liked his hobby. It wasn't everyone you could take up on a hill on a chilly night.

Sometimes the seeing was awful, but tonight's was reasonable. And the moon was always a gift, best at less than full, where the terminator, the division between light and dark, threw shadows in the craters nearby.

'Start with Copernicus then,' he conceded. 'And then follow through to...' He looked at his map of the moon brightened by his red light torch. 'To Plato.'

Mia went to the eyepiece on the side of the scope. It was about her height; she barely had to bend.

'Oh there it is, Copernicus, almost in the middle, the terminator just touching the west of it. I wish we had a bigger scope...'

'Wouldn't be able to carry it,' he said.

'And then to the north east of it, at the tip of the Apennine mountains, there's that long one I can never remember the name of...'

Neither could Jack who looked at his map. 'Eratosthenes.'

'Why do they have to give craters such strange names?'

'Don't know. Call it Mia.'

'Yes!' She clapped her hands together. 'There's crater Mia at the tip of the Apennines, named after the famous girl astronomer, then following the ridge as it curves round – and there we have crater Jack...' She took a sly look at her dad. 'Also known as Archimedes. Which has two little ones just to the north of it, and I don't know the names of them...'

'Alison and ...'

'Jack?' she suggested.

'We've already had Jack,' he said. 'And anyway, they wouldn't be together.'

She came off the scope.

'I don't want to go to Brighton,' she said.

'It's got the sea and cliffs and lots of life.'

She shook her head. 'It hasn't got my friends. It hasn't got you.'

'You can still stay with me alternate weekends.'

'But not odd days like this.'

'No,' he had to admit. That would be impossible. Picking her up at 3.30, taking her back to his place 70 miles away, then getting her to school in the morning, wasn't on. It'd be all driving, with an afternoon's work thrown away and the next morning's too.

'Can I come and live with you?' she said.

'Your mum is prime carer,' he said. 'She wouldn't agree.' And he wasn't sure he wanted it, but didn't say. Though Alison was working full time and managed. Managed because she could call on him when she was going out on a date. But that wouldn't happen in Brighton.

'She hasn't got the job yet,' he added. 'So it could all come to nothing.'

'I hope so.'

He looked at his watch. 'We can only stay another 15 minutes. Find the Sea of Tranquillity.'

'Stop asking me all the easy ones.' She turned to him. 'You know my teacher, Miss Brown? She didn't know what the terminator was.'

'I bet your mum doesn't either. And she's a teacher too.'

'Yes she does. I told her. And also, you know what my teacher said?'

'Tell me.'

'This is dead dumb. She said there was no gravity on the moon.'

Jack laughed, imagining what his daughter would say to that.

'And what did you say?'

'I put my hand up and said – yes, there is. It's a sixth of Earth's.'

'What did she say to that, clever sticks?'

Attempting an imitation of her teacher, she said, 'There's no gravity on the moon, Mia. And I'll talk to you at playtime.' In her own voice she added, 'And she did. I almost got a telling off, till we checked it on Wikipedia. And I was right. And she said – oh I meant atmosphere.'

'Don't get too smart. You won't be popular.'

'But she was wrong.'

'Don't tell her in front of the whole class. Tell her on her own. Anyway, back to the Sea of Tranquillity. Take us south to Clavius.'

'I can't do that, there's millions of craters in that direction, Dad.'

'Find one you like amongst them.'

'I know, I know one,' she said eagerly, looking through the scope. 'There. Alphonsus. It's got a little house in the middle.'

'I don't think it's a house.'

'Yes, the man in the moon lives there. And the cow comes to visit. Oh look there, she's coming now. Wow!' She came off the scope. 'That was a shooting star.'

'It'll bring you luck.'

'Then I won't be going to Brighton!'

She did a spin and a high five with Jack.

Chapter 15

Frank was in The Goose in Stratford Broadway with Bert. The light was dim with small, fake coach lights along the side walls. The pub was their chosen watering hole, better than the poncy Goldengrove up the road, which was too full of social workers and liberal wankers.

He couldn't stop waggling his tooth with his tongue. It was going to come out pretty soon, hanging by a string of flesh. And maybe he'd live with the gap, instead of dental work. He hated dentists, being helpless in that chair. His eye stung. It'd probably be black in the morning. The nose bleed he was able to staunch at home, and felt as if he'd done fifteen rounds and been KO'd at the bell.

Bert handed him his second pint.

'He can't get away with it,' said Bert, obviously thinking while at the bar.

Frank took a sip, and grimaced. It went right in the tooth. He tried a sip on the other side and that was better.

'He can't, he bloody well can't,' exclaimed Frank. 'They have to learn whose country this is.'

Bert was tall and thin with a generous bubbling of ginger hair. His skin was whitish pink, as if he'd been laying out on his father's refrigerated butcher's slab in Manor Park. He worked in his father's shop along with a sister. All three stalwarts of the local chapter of England First.

'Petrol through the letterbox, followed by a match?' suggested Bert. 'Quick and low risk.'

'If you don't bloody well live in the house. I'm on the second floor, Bert, and they're up above on the third, so I'd go first.' He waved away the idea. 'No fire, mate. Let's get more creative.'

Frank wondered about Bert. You could always get him on side for a good kicking but he was inclined to be impulsive, and didn't always think. You had the goal, sure, but a big part of it was not getting caught. He'd have to be the brains in this.

'Pity,' said Bert. 'I do like a bit of fire. I mean even if they know it's arson, how can they pin it on you unless they've seen you pouring in the petrol. But I take the point, you don't want to destroy your own house, so dump that. Are you thinking both of 'em or just the one?'

The music had struck up loud, some fierce drumming and guitar riffs. Frank for a few seconds was irritated, but then realised it was no bad thing, as who could overhear them through this racket. He pulled his chair closer to Bert's.

'I was considering that when you were getting the pint,' he said almost in his ear. 'My first thought was go for the nigger. But then I thought there's millions of them. What's the point? But his bitch is pregnant with his kid...'

'We should discourage fraternisation,' added Bert helpfully.

Frank nodded and rubbed his jaw. 'Fucking tooth. I'll make 'em sorry they ever took me on. I'm gonna keep my eye on her for a couple of days. See where she works. Her timings. I know she's got a motor. I've seen her come and go in it. Why don't you come over for tea, day after tomorrow. Say half five. Bessie'll cook us up something.'

'I'll bring some steak from the shop.'

'That'll be great. This tooth'll be out by then if I have to do it myself with pincers. She can cook it. Onions, mushrooms, chips with your steak. Have a good feed up, I'll get some beers in. Then I'll get rid of her. Send her off to the pictures or something, and we can work out what we do with the bitch. You still got that little place up Epping?'

'Yeh, going there next week to do a bit of fishing.'

'Might prove useful for a bigger catch, mate.'

Chapter 16

Anne was looking out of her French windows into the dark garden. The light from the room spilled out across the lawn, gradually fading into black. She couldn't make out the shed or the tree at the back at all. Though sometimes when Clapton United were training at night, the floodlights spilled and she could hear the yelling. The ground was just beyond the back of her garden, its entrance by the Spotted Dog. Such a sad boarded up place. Henry VIII was said to hunt from there. But she'd never known it in use. Locals told her it'd been a lovely pub with a restaurant, Irish music, and then somehow lost it when the manager left.

She liked her French windows, the light they gave her during the day, the easy access to the garden, but once the footballers turned off their floodlights at night, the gloom was frightening. Windows were fragile, the lock not that good. Living on the ground floor had its rewards but also its dangers, especially for a woman on her own.

She drew the long, orange curtains. And shuddered at the thought of the fight. She was seated next to Frank when David threw the punch. And then, in the mêlée, she was avoiding boots and fists and crockery. It was only by luck she wasn't collateral damage. The speed of it shocked her. Admittedly, Frank was pushing for it, and something had to happen. David could have called the police, should have, you might say, but Frank with his 'half-caste, abortion' hectoring, his challenge by sitting it out, hadn't given David much of a choice.

If only she hadn't been quite so close to the action.

She seemed to attract violence. There was Malcolm, always Malcolm. She often came back to him, late evenings on her own. Finding him all but dead when she returned from her supposed evening class, blood all over the sitting room where his failing body had crawled. Then the police and the dreadful aftermath.

This was her new life, bought with the insurance. She sat on the little table in the nursery. How long could she keep this up for? The days were long. The baby came at 7.30 in the morning, and wasn't picked up till 6.30 in the evening. You wondered why the parents had a child at all, but she couldn't question her paymasters. A servant in effect. And one lot of kids would be replaced by another lot, until the last syllable of recorded time. No, this had to be a temporary halt, say a couple of years, while this time she actually did the evening class.

It had seemed perfect then. She'd enrolled for a modular arts degree, part time at the local college, three evenings a week. Showed Malcolm the receipt and everything. What a wonderful plan! Except it grew more complicated. She had to lie about the course, make up tutors, even buying books to make it look real, while she was romping with Steve in that tiny flat of his.

The lies, the strain of making them up was almost degree level, the desperate sex and the sudden halt with the murder. She'd ended up with no qualifications, other than widow. Fierce and kinky sex, and so what? It was addictive, painful and pointless. She might as well have been sticking needles in her arm. There was little love in it, would you even call it need? Any more than you need whisky or cocaine.

Or anything, if it comes to that.

This was going to be another sleepless night. Dwelling on her Malcolm days, the lies she'd told him while dripping with sex. Think about tomorrow, slam shut the past. The builder, for whom she was going to make dinner. Might there not be a chance there? Some civilised relationship. He seemed a nice, companionable man, a little sad, but she could hardly complain. No booze, no bad thing considering her own problems there.

And they would settle down, have a child or two, buy a house in the suburbs, she'd do an Open University degree in something or other, paint and grow vegetables and keep chickens. There, she'd married him already and not even had the first date.

It was easy to do that with someone you didn't know. Far easier than with someone you did.

Don't be overeager. That sets them running. Don't sleep together on the first date. Had she blown that one, asking him to dinner here? But at 35, with the new feminism, can you really hang about waiting to be asked?

Such a bundle of insecurities. She needed to work with someone, instead of on her own. To be able to discuss things, plan things. Instead she was stuck singing songs to toddlers.

But it was a job. These days, no small thing.

Count your blessings: she was her own boss instead of some bastard busybody over her, her own flat, healthy, and a date tomorrow night. Count them and forget Malcolm and the blood trails in the sitting room, and the lies you told him, and the sex games with Steve that simply made you feel worse about your betrayal.

Like Marley's ghost she'd dragged her chains and cash boxes the 200 miles south to East London.

A cup of tea, some marmite on toast. And see if she can find a late night film worth watching.

Chapter 17

Bessie couldn't sleep. His snoring made it difficult enough, but it was hard to get comfortable with her bruised shoulder where he'd thumped her when they'd got back after the non-meeting in the upstairs flat. She should have supported him, he'd yelled. But how could she have said anything when she was eating their cake and drinking their tea? They were always nice to her. She didn't care what colour their baby would be. Besides, it's hard to speak up with so many people.

Ten years ago, she might have hated David. Not just for being black. She'd done a lot of hating at school. The black boys were rough and they teased her. But so did the white boys. They were a dirty lot too. The black girls were OK, always getting in trouble with their short skirts and cheek. The Asian girls were always talking about weddings. And she never got on with the white girls, they teased her too for her small breasts and bad teeth.

What with the kids and the teachers, she was glad to leave school.

Since then she'd turned about. Hated other people less. It came with her increasing hatred of Frank once her mother had run off. She told everyone she was dead; that stopped them asking about her. But now she was her replacement. His sex and punch bag. Tonight he'd come in drunk, so he was quick. Better that way, then off to sleep and snoring.

She lay on the edge of the bed; he had three quarters of it. In the morning, quite often she could avoid sex if she got up sharpish and made his breakfast. Though sometimes that tactic simply delayed things to post-breakfast.

Tonight the box was under the bed. More or less where

his heart was. There was no way he could have spotted it, coming in so drunk. The ingredients were energised by the spell she and Nancy had pronounced. And now its magic would seep out over the hours of the night, and soak the foul soul of her father.

And so seal his fate.

She had the feeling this one would work. She'd found it online, though she was always getting graphic pop-ups from his porn sites. She'd learnt to ignore them. They were there, like wallpaper. Besides, the more he wanked to screen fantasies, the less he had for her. The site told her the spell was dangerous, said when it had been used before and its effects. She had tried other ones, but they never worked. This one had a history.

It was the darkest of black magic.

Then she would be free. Not his punchbag and post pub comforter. She wondered where her mother was, what she was doing. And resented her for not taking her with, but leaving her to him. So she became his wife and tormented servant, instead of her mum.

Her mum might as well be dead. For all the good she'd done her.

The only thing she owed her was the flowerbed that her mother had kept up and she'd taken over. She'd worried when she saw what the builder was going to do, but her plants were going to be alright. He was doing his best. She'd already put the first ones back, where the builder had taken the broken bit of wall away. Watered them in and they hadn't wilted. He was nice; he listened to her. She'd like to be his wife. She'd asked him if he was married and he said he wasn't, though he had a daughter. She didn't mind that but wished he didn't talk to Anne so much. Anne had her eye on him, that was obvious.

Could she go in the sitting room and sleep? But then if he woke up he'd simply yell for her and hit her one. Though she could say she'd simply gone to the toilet but he might hit her one anyway. Just in case, he would say.

Thank God he had his taxi. What hell her life would be if he were unemployed. The less she saw of him the better. He had some regular work quite early in the morning, taking a kid to school somewhere in Woodford. She hoped he didn't lose that. It was her free time. Quite often until lunchtime as he got other fares.

Tomorrow night, well not tomorrow anymore, tonight, she and Nancy had to complete the spell by burying the box by moonlight. She'd seen the moon tonight, on the way to a full moon. So tomorrow at midnight. Completion. She just hoped he'd be drunk or out with the cab or anywhere but here.

Please work, she prayed.

Chapter 18

Rainy morning. You always got extra work on rainy days. Everyone wanted a cab. But this morning, he had other things to do. Besides, he'd worked practically all of the last seven days, so he deserved it. The car needed a clean out, so might as well be today. He'd get Bessie on it when he got back.

The wipers swished the screen, clarifying it for an instant before it began to blotch over again. That didn't make it easy following someone. Especially with rush hour traffic. Stratford High Street was murder at the best of times. But he mustn't get too close or she'd spot him. Or too far away as he'd lose her. He should've got a black car, this orange was too easy to pick out. But when you buy second hand, colour is not top of the list.

Quite a few jars he and Bert had downed last night. Couldn't face breakfast, the usual sausages, beans and egg. Told Bessie to bin it. Good to talk to his mucker, someone civilised, who knew what was what. And he needed the beers after that fight with that black bastard. His tooth was still hanging by a string of flesh and his eye was black. But the matter was in hand. Bert and he would do for him and his missus.

Maggie was on the right hand side, into the slip for Carpenters Road, maybe heading for Hackney Marshes, that way anyway. He got into the lane, stopped at the traffic lights as she was. And waited. She wasn't going anywhere for the moment.

He'd given Bessie another smack this morning for not supporting him at the meeting. The two others had kept quiet, mind you. Nancy, well he could expect no more of her and her half dead moggie. He had plans for that too. But Anne, she'd never said anything. Full, fleshy bit of work, conveniently downstairs. He'd never seen her with anyone, so maybe he should visit and see if he could change her attitude.

The lights changed and he was just able to get round before they were against him. Less congested here. Lots of old factories cleared out for the Olympic Games. There was the Olympic Stadium and that Paki's twisted, scrap metal whatjercallit. He was crossing and recrossing the river Lea, never quite sure which bit was which. In a few minutes, he was into what he called the arty farty sector of Hackney Wick. He'd clear 'em all out. Wastrels most of 'em. Living off benefits. Best keep fairly close, with all the mess of roads this side of Victoria Park, easy to lose someone.

His thoughts returned to Anne. Bessie was boring, passive, had to be threatened to do anything. And she wasn't much anyway. Just there. A fill in, while he waited for someone like her downstairs. There, any day of the week and twice on Sundays.

Why wait?

He knew this area. Homerton, heading north from Victoria Park. Traffic lights coming up, better keep close watch. She was on the green and turning into Homerton High Street, by the old Hackney Hospital. This could be tricky; he'd have to beat the lights. Or she'd get away.

He zipped round with the lights barely on yellow, going red as he came past. But he was there amid the hooting. Cab driving had taught him aggressive driving. Still, that was chancy. But he could see her, a little way up, in clear view. Concentrate, mate, lay off the fantasies with her downstairs, or he'd lose Maggie in a quick turn off.

Bert's place in Epping. Perfect. So out of the way, you could scream and not even the deer would look up. Concentrate. She was turning.

Down a side road. Someone else just ahead was turning

too, a builder's van. *Jack of All Trades* – he's the guy working on the house. What's he doing up here?

As Frank turned, he saw Maggie's car a little way down the road turning off into a school driveway. The builder's van ahead of him pulled up at the side of the road, and Frank drove past. Marshland Primary School, he noted the sign. Then, perhaps 50 yards further on, he pulled up himself. He was curious about the builder. Could he also be watching Maggie? If so, he'd better find out why or they'd be treading on each other's toes.

Frank pulled up and got out of the car. Lots of kids and parents on the pavement, both sides of the road. And all the cars from the school run. He'd been lucky to get a spot. The rain was teeming down, wetting his neck and remnant of hair, running down his face. He was about to dive back in the vehicle when he saw the builder get out of his van. He was with a schoolgirl who had an umbrella up. He was holding her hand as he crossed the road with her, saw her to the school gate and waved her in.

A proud dad. There we go. Coincidence. Leave now, best not to be seen by the builder as he'd find it difficult to say why he was here. Dropping off a fare, he'd have to say, something like that. Coincidence only stretched so far.

He climbed back in the car and was quickly away. Next on the list: mincemeat and tacks. He had plans for a cat.

Chapter 19

Jack spent half an hour in a café on Woodgrange Road, just down from Forest Gate Station. Very local, he was a regular. This morning he had his usual, a bacon sandwich and large mug of tea, hoping the rain would stop. The windows were steamed up, and he could barely see outside although he had a window seat, but knew it was still raining from the state of those coming in. The café was quite full, mostly workmen, watching the weather like himself, eating greasy food and reading tabloids or chatting noisily about last night's game. He finished his Mirror, drained the last of his tea. Maybe he did need a better paper; something with more meat. He worked on his own, so who cared what he read?

Except the Guardian was Alison's paper. Forget that then. And no way the Times or the Telegraph. Papers for toffs. Could try the Independent. Except you get used to a paper – and giving up the Mirror would be like abandoning an old friend.

The rain wasn't going to stop. And so with reluctance, he went back out into the flurry, and drove to the house, along Woodgrange, across the Romford Road to Upton Lane. The traffic was slow, rain always did this, stop, start. Then round the bend and past the sad old Spotted Dog. That used to be such a good pub. Even giving up drinking, he could regret its dilapidated state. Tiles were coming off the roof, the white weatherboard siding shifting in places. Before you knew it, there'd be wet rot and dry rot, and another bit of history lost to ruin.

He turned into Ham Park Road, and, once he'd parked, staying in the van, put on his overalls. Kitted up, he got out and took his sledgehammer from the back. The full skip had been taken away. Good. They were a reliable firm, but you could never be sure. And an empty one had been left, except someone had already put a mattress in it. He thought of chucking it out, but never liked it when people dumped stuff on the streets, so wouldn't do it himself. He hoped there'd be enough room for the remnant of the wall.

He went in by the garden gate, noting the wheelbarrow that he'd left by the wall upside down. He'd hardly taken half a dozen steps in when Bessie ran out from the shed at the back of the garden.

'I've moved the plants already for the next bit,' she said eagerly.

Her hair was soaked, the lengths straggly down her face. Her dress clung to her.

'Bessie,' he said sternly, 'you don't have to be out in this weather.'

'I've got to look after my plants,' she said defensively.

'Well, now you're ahead, get in the shed for half an hour. Or go upstairs in the dry.'

'Do you want a cup of tea?' she said brightly.

He didn't, except it'd get her out of the rain. But would that mean he'd have to keep drinking tea until the rain stopped?

'I don't want you catching pneumonia,' he said.

'I won't.'

He shook his head at her petulance. What to do? He didn't want to shout at her. Then he had a thought. He had hardly any food in the house.

'Will you run an errand for me?'

'Yeh, course,' she said eagerly.

He took her to the van. And in the dry made up a grocery list. He handed it over with a twenty pound note.

'Now go and get a coat and a shopping bag.'

She skipped off. He was glad to be free of her for a while, and went back to work. There was nothing for it but to get a soaking. No one was paying him wet time. He'd have to grin and bear it. Putting on his goggles and gloves, he set to at hammering the wall, the rain coming down steadily.

Having carted away two barrowfuls, he was returning through the garden gate when he saw a portly, middle-aged man in the garden. Whatever was he up to on the lawn, walking about, eyes down, and dropping things? Jack stopped, put down the barrow and watched. There was a furtiveness about him. Having dropped a few of whatever it was, he took more out of his jacket pocket and dropped some more every few yards.

Distinctly odd.

Jack picked up the barrow handles and began whistling to alert the man, as if he hadn't seen anything. Then wheeled in to the bit of wall where he was working.

The man, alerted, came over. He was attempting to smile through bad teeth. He had quite a black eye.

'Hello,' he said, 'I'm Frank. Bessie's dad.'

He put out his hand. Jack took a glove off and shook it.

'Jack,' he said. 'Doing some building work for you all.'

Frank looked at the wall thoughtfully, as if he knew about these things. 'Doing well there. Had to go, leaning like the fucking Tower of Pisa.'

'I was hoping to finish the demolition today,' said Jack, 'and put the fence in tomorrow, but this rain...'

'Seems to be easing off,' said Frank looking up at the sky.

Jack didn't think it was, but you never could tell. Then he remembered.

'Didn't I see you up Marshland school?'

Frank shook his head forcefully, 'No, wasn't me. Never heard of the place.'

It was you, thought Jack, I've seen your orange Aurora out front. But why push it?

'You haven't seen my daughter, Bessie, have you?'

'Well,' said Jack, not sure how this would be taken. 'I sent her off to buy some groceries for me. Sorry if I shouldn't have.'

'That's fine, mate,' said Frank quickly, tapping him on the shoulder. 'I like to see her busy. Idleness only gets you fat. I'll be upstairs in the flat. When she gets back, send her up.'

'Will do,' said Jack.

Frank wandered off to the back door of the house. Jack shook the water out of his hair, he'd obviously interrupted Frank in whatever he was doing; he'd have a look in a minute. Jack dumped some lumps of broken brickwork in the barrow. And, when he was sure the man was safely inside, Jack had a look on the lawn. And there, he picked up a raw meatball, about the size of a marble. He squashed it between his fingers. Inside was a half inch tack.

Jack went back to work, reflecting. He continued filling the wheelbarrow. Once full, he wheeled it out to the skip in the roadway. There, he'd set up a long plank leaning against the skip. He ran the barrow up and tipped it in the skip. Dangerous, he knew, especially in this weather, but it saved time. One tip and it was all in. As he strolled back with the empty barrow, he thought why would you put a tack in a meatball? Because of who might eat it, obviously. He could think of no other reason. A crow might eat it, or a dog or a cat. The animal might swallow the tack or it might get stuck in its throat, which was surely the intention.

He looked up at the windows of the house. The man might be watching him. Well, so what? It was a heartless way to kill anything.

He went up and down the lawn, picking up meatballs. At first, he took out the tack and tossed the meatball away, but when he began picking up empty meatballs, he realised he had to gather them all up or he wouldn't know which was which.

A little later, Bessie returned with the shopping. She had Sainsbury's shopping bags hanging from each hand and looked pleased with herself. She wore a thin plastic raincoat, which probably didn't do her much good at keeping out the rain as she was thoroughly wet already, but perhaps kept her marginally warmer.

He took the shopping and change from her, and gave her a two pound coin.

'Thank you,' she said with a smile. 'You don't have to.'

He couldn't help liking her, she was just like a child really, so eager to please. So easy to offend.

'It means I'll have some food in the house. Thanks a lot, Bessie,' he said. 'And oh yes, your dad's upstairs and he wants you.'

She gasped, her hands flying to her cheeks.

'It's alright,' he said, a hand on her arm, 'he told me it was no problem you doing some shopping for me.'

She was dancing on the spot as if in pain.

'He'll go bananas!'

And she was off running to the house.

Chapter 20

The rain continued through the morning. Jack felt like an abused carthorse, but the only whip was his own. He could of course sit it out in the dry somewhere; he was his own boss, but he'd be that much poorer when it came to the reckoning as he was paid by the job, not by the hours.

His hair, shirt and trousers were soaked through. At least his feet had stayed dry, a decent pair of boots paid off, his hands were protected by the gloves, but the rest of him was a chilly layer of wet. And the sky a dark grey with no sign of a break.

He was wiping the goggles which kept watering over, when there came a shout from the house.

'Do you want a cup of tea, Jack?'

He glanced over to see Anne at the French windows, open just enough for her to poke her head out.

'Love one,' and he strode across.

She opened the windows wider. Jack looked down at his muddy boots.

'Best take them off,' he said.

He sat down on the patio and removed his boots, and then stepped into her nursery, carrying the boots. The children were playing, but Anne had gone off somewhere. Then she was back with a towel. Jack put his boots down by the door and closed the window.

Anne threw him the towel.

'Dry yourself off.'

It was a thick, white bath towel, still warm from the airing cupboard. He began vigorously rubbing his hair and face. It was a relief to get some heat into them. Then his neck and arms, which was as much as he could get to.

'I've got a kettle on,' she said.

She felt his shirt.

'You are absolutely drenched.'

Her hand stayed, and his folded over it. He pulled her to him and they embraced, and slipped into a kiss. There was no resistance. She was warm against his chill, her lips greedy. Eyes closed, his fingers explored her firm neck.

A cry from the baby broke them apart.

'Will you make the tea?' she said with a helpless gesture, 'everything's in the kitchen.'

She went to the playpen where the baby was standing against the side, holding onto the bars and crying for whatever babies cry for. Comfort, warmth, the same human needs. Pointless resenting his cry, although Jack couldn't help it. Competition. He recalled Mia as a baby; as a screaming toddler, the best contraceptive ever.

Jack went into the kitchen. It was tidy and clean. Probably had to be, for inspections. He had no trouble finding things. The tea was in a caddy labelled tea, the teapot already emptied. The first cupboard he opened, over the sink, had mugs. He poured the hot water in the pot, reflecting on what had just happened. He had been kissed. Or rather he had kissed her, but she had wanted it as much as he had.

He didn't get many tea breaks like this.

He put milk in the cups, and leaving the tea to brew, went back out to the nursery. She had given the twins milk and apple, while the baby was contently sucking from a bottle, half sitting, leaning against a corner of the playpen, reminiscent of an elderly alcoholic. She came back to him and put an arm round his waist as she surveyed the short term peace of the nursery.

He said, 'What do you know about Frank?'

'Other than I don't like him,' she said. 'And that he treats his daughter dreadfully. Not much. Why do you want to know?'

He told her about the meatballs with the tacks inside.

'Are there any animals in the house?' he said.

'Nancy has a cat...' A hand went to her mouth. 'He wouldn't. He couldn't.'

'I'm afraid he has.'

She turned to him. 'Shall we call the police?'

He shook his head. 'They'd probably regard it as trivial. He'd say it was for crows or squirrels...'

'It's for Nancy's cat,' she said. 'I know it.'

'And another thing...' he said, then interrupted himself. 'Let's get the tea.'

He led the way into the kitchen, she followed part of the way, staying half out to keep an eye on the children.

'My daughter Mia stayed with me last night,' he said as he poured out the tea. 'And I took her to school this morning, Marshland Primary. And he was there. Frank. I've seen that orange car of his out here. But when I saw him in the garden, and said I'd seen him at the school, he denied it. And changed the subject dead sharp.'

'Marshland?' exclaimed Anne. 'That's Maggie's school.'

'Who's Maggie?'

'She and David have the top flat. Oh, I'm getting a bad feeling.'

She told him about last night's meeting and its aftermath.

'That accounts for the black eye,' he said. 'Why would he follow her?'

'No good reason,' said Anne. 'Especially if he's denied being there.'

They took their teas out to the nursery. She warned him to keep his mug well away from the children, to put it on a high shelf if he went anywhere near them.

'I'm going to tell David and Maggie,' she said. 'Let them decide if they want to call the police.'

'Probably best,' he said. 'Must get on.'

He threw back the last of the tea. She took his cup and held his fingers. He stared into her blue eyes, she looked back, her lips parted, expectant. Jack shook himself, he felt uncomfortable in a nursery.

'Better earn some money.'

Jack went to the window, sat down on the floor and pulled his boots on.

'Is there anything you don't eat?' she said. 'Tonight's meal.'

'I can't stand sprouts and sour cream.'

She smiled. 'Neither of those are on the menu. Seven thirty, right?'

'Right.'

He stood up. They embraced.

'You can come back here for lunch,' she said.

He shook his head. 'Love to, but I've got to go to the merchants and order fencing and posts for tomorrow.'

'Then it's tonight,' she said. 'Free of children and work.'

'Tonight,' he said, and stepped out into the rain.

Chapter 21

Bessie had a walloping for not being at home when her father got back. He walloped her again because she was snivelling as she made his lunch. And might have walloped her again if she had not eaten with him, which she would much rather not as she could barely eat in his company. But she consented out of necessity, sitting opposite him and forcing down some food. He told her off for having a grizzly face. How could he eat opposite that? he asked. It was a penance. She couldn't put on a smile for him. Though she tried, but it was such a poor thing that he made her stand in the corner while he told her how a proper daughter should stand, behave, and what he wanted from her in future. Or she was for it.

'And another thing. I don't want you talking to that builder. He's a busybody. Paid to work, not to gossip with you. And why are you running errands for him?'

Because he's nice to me, she might have said if she wasn't afraid of a walloping. Please, die, she thought as she followed a crack in the wall with her finger. Get in a car crash, have a heart attack. Anything, just leave me be, as the tears rolled down and caught in the side of her mouth.

'If you'd have been here,' he went on, 'you could have cleaned the car out. The car that keeps you, don't you forget it. You're just like your fucking mother, the pair of you, a waste of space. Everything's so grudging. Now, I have to be out and working. Someone has to. Don't know why I put up with you. How many times must I tell you – keep your phone with you. Forget again and you'll get a right seeing to. I'll phone when I'm on the way back. Maybe six. Dinner ready. Get me a couple of chops. Not for you. You don't deserve it.'

He slapped a five pound note on the table.

In the corner she poked out her tongue. She should've run away years ago, but where would she go without money or friends? The only people she knew were here. Nancy was kind to her, and Tickles sat in her lap. Maggie always had a nice word. And so had the builder. She'd like to marry him, but her father would kill her if she said another word to him.

Frank left, slamming the door behind him. She stayed in the corner until she heard the front door close. Then, and only then, she turned carefully around, just in case he was tricking her. But he had gone. And she sank into a chair with relief, wiping her eyes with her sleeve.

A little later, she was sick in the toilet. She couldn't help it. It was forcing down food that she didn't want, his food, in front of him. If only she could find where her mum was. But there had not been a word in ten years.

She washed her hands and face. Then did the washing up. She didn't mind doing chores when he wasn't here. The warm sudsy water was soothing. She'd best go off and buy the chops. Or she'd never know the end of it if she forgot. No way. And take her phone with, just in case he calls. Then, only then, she'd go and see Nancy, empty the cat litter. Have a stroke of Tickles and take him out into the garden, never mind the rain.

It didn't lecture you or belt you. And was good for the skin.

Except she mustn't talk to the builder. Or not be caught anyway. All she'd done was run an errand for him. One errand. And he gave her two pounds. Which showed he liked her. She must look for a love spell on the computer while her dad was out. He mustn't catch her at it. No way. Find one, write it out. Then get the ingredients.

She'd like to be a builder's wife. Keep the house clean

while he was at work, do all the shopping, make breakfast and dinner for him. Do his laundry. Have a baby and two cats, a black one and a white one. Put his washing out on the line on blowy days, and iron it while waiting for him to come home.

Her father would be dead. Finishing the spell tonight would take care of that. It had to. Then she'd get him cremated. Burn every last bone of him.

And drop his ashes in the cat litter – and let Tickles poo on him.

Chapter 22

Nancy hadn't slept well last night. Her shoulder hurt where she'd fallen in the supermarket. And while tossing about, she kept thinking about the row at the meeting, or rather what was supposed to be a meeting. All that flying china, fists and boots. She was glad David had given Frank a good hiding. But she didn't think it would end there, these things never did.

She could never sleep during the day. She'd tried this afternoon but had been woken by Bessie yelling. He was hitting her again, up there in the sitting room above hers. She always knew. Every time she thought of calling the police, but he would know who called them. And he would come down here. And what could she do? In the supermarket, she'd been pathetic.

How she hated growing old!

Millie had come. It was so pleasant to have a visitor. She thought her quite heroic considering the dreadful weather.

'Three buses I had to catch,' exclaimed Millie. 'The one from Barkingside came straight away, so I got on, and of course then I'd committed myself, hadn't I? The next one, either an 25 or 86 at Ilford, I waited ages for. Normally they're so frequent. I don't know what was the matter today. And thought of giving up, but I'd missed one going back – so waited until at last an 86 came. And it was so packed, that I had to stand all the way to the Princess Alice. And young people these days never give up a seat to an elderly person. I blame their parents. No manners, playing with their phones. And then, when I got off, I had to stand around in the rain to catch a 325 to the Spotted Dog. That is such a useless service. Might as well have walked. Couldn't have got any wetter.'

Millie moaned a lot which made Nancy think she must do it herself. But wasn't that old age for you? Everything was more difficult and no one took any notice of you. And what could you do for yourself? And what with everyone so slow, home helps, doctors, meals-on-wheels... She was determined not to moan at Bessie, the poor girl tried her best. He hit her for nothing. Last thing she needed was another telling off. Though she was late taking out the cat litter. And had to do it when Millie was here. She hated that when she had a visitor.

'The girl tries hard,' she said to Millie when Bessie was out emptying the litter tray. 'Her father hits her and I don't know what else. But she's a nice girl in her way, always helpful to me. So don't say anything when she comes back.'

'She should have her teeth seen to,' said Millie.

'Times I've told her that,' said Nancy, 'either she's scared, or her father won't let her. He's a nasty bully, pushed me over in the supermarket, but bit off more than he could chew last night – and David upstairs beat him up. Didn't he wallop him one! I almost wanted to join in. He kicks Tickles every time he sees him. Yet Bessie, his daughter, is as nice as pie.'

Bessie came back. Nancy wondered whether she'd been listening at the door. And thought of what she'd said. Depended how long Bessie'd been listening in. But then again, she hadn't said anything nasty.

'Will you pour the tea out, love?'

The tea was on the sideboard with the cake and crockery. Bessie poured out two cups and then put the milk in. Nancy was going to say you should put the milk in first, but thought no, I mustn't keep telling her off. And I should leave her some money in my will. Though only if I can stop her father getting his hands on it.

'One sugar for you, Nancy,' as Bessie gave her the cup

and saucer. 'And none for you, Millie.'

'I'm sweet enough already,' said Millie with a little giggle.

Nancy heard this every time. She didn't mind. It was well meant. Besides, she liked company, and Millie made all this effort to come and see her. Three buses. Though she wondered how much longer.

'Do you both want cake?' said Bessie.

They did. Bessie carefully cut two slices of the coffee cream cake.

'Don't you want a piece yourself?' said Nancy.

'Go on,' said Millie, 'you're all skin and bone.'

Bessie smiled at them and said, 'I've not long had my lunch. So I'm not hungry now. Thank you very much, Nancy.'

'Then have some tea at least.'

'I will,' she said. And poured herself a cup.

'Has your dad gone out, Bessie?' said Nancy.

'Yes, he's out with the cab this afternoon.'

'That's good,' said Nancy.

'Yes, it is,' said Bessie.

They both knew what they meant by that, but didn't want to make it plain in front of Millie.

A little later Bessie said, 'The rain seems to be stopping. Can I take Tickles out in the back garden?'

'Yes, dear. But do keep an eye on him. You know what that horrible ginger cat's like.'

'Thank you, Nancy. I'll look after him. Promise.'

And she picked Tickles up in her arms and took him outside, leaving Millie and Nancy free to discuss the scandal of the house, much of which involved Bessie's father.

Chapter 23

Maggie was ironing. A few blouses for herself, a couple of shirts for David – that would do. Just enough to keep up, though she must put a wash on. That would annoy him downstairs, anyone else she might have been more conciliatory – but let the machine shake his ceiling down. The busyness of the school day had kept last night out of her head, but as soon as she was back within her own four walls, the events renewed themselves. Frank's insults and the fight. David had thrown the first punch but she was with him all the way. All those racial insults and Frank's refusal to leave. You wanted to come home to peace and quiet after the hectic demands of the working day, but beneath your feet, as you ate, washed your clothes and relaxed, lived a hateful man.

She resented her thoughts being taken over by him. No wonder the very rich had huge estates with large fields and high walls guarding the boundaries. And great iron gates. All to keep the enemy at bay. Not marauding Vikings these days but those with a different world view.

Only people like us may enter.

She was going to have a black baby. Of course it was half white, so logically you could say it was a white baby – but it didn't work that way. A smidgen of black genes and you were black. Actually mixed race. Oh those dreadful dividers! The peering eyes, sizing you up, boxing you up. Frank was right in a way. She, David and their child would have a constant battle, would have to continually face up to a prejudiced world. Was it fair, he'd said, bringing a child into this world. A world with too many people like me, he might have added.

The thought exhausted her. The years of upbringing, the mothers at the school gate. And her daughter who would need to stand up for herself in the playground. Maggie fiercely ironed a sleeve and shirt front. Well, she would fight her corner, mostly seeing a daughter, though admitting there was only a 50% chance. She, yes a she, would come out of a strong family, one where she was loved – so she knew who she was.

In the end it didn't matter; you had to fight all your life anyway, to hold onto your values in a sea of cheap and nasty flotsam. Get rich capitalism and flag-waving patriotism.

It would be nice to come home and not think like this. But this was the real world, and there would be tears and fights. Mind you, next time they moved they'd interrogate the neighbours. And what a waste of time that would be! All jolly with their tea cups, until you moved in.

There was nothing else for it. She needed a 500 acre estate, a mile long driveway and walls twenty feet high. Each night the Rottweilers would be out, kept half starved, and the key to the gun cabinet in her purse.

All from that rat downstairs. Stop, stop, stop. Put a kettle on. David would be back shortly.

She folded the ironing and put it away. And the board and iron. The kettle went on and she did half an hour's marking before David arrived, with easy jazz playing in the background.

David came. They had a quick embrace and she went to make tea. He followed her into the kitchen and patted her bump as she filled the kettle.

'What's it like in there?' he said.

'Dark, and I've nothing to read,' said Maggie in a squeaky voice.

'That's not Yoruba,' said David.

'She's bilingual.'

'Clever boy!' he said.

She blew a raspberry at him.

He said, 'Careful now. You are directing non verbal abuse against the area manager.'

'So you told them?'

'I said, my wife says I've got to take it. And I have no say in the matter.'

'I didn't say that,' she said offended.

He pecked her on the cheek.

'I know you didn't, dear. I'm just feeling resentful at this fucking propertied world, where I have taken a job I don't want so we can get a house – and will yes sir, no sir, for the next 25 years so I don't lose my job, and we can pay for it.'

'You don't have to do that,' she said.

'And how might we make it work otherwise, my wise wife?'

She ignored the putdown and said, 'I go back to work as soon as I can after the baby is born. You have another go at getting articled to a solicitor's.'

'I tried for two years,' he said between his teeth: 'Two damn years with nothing on my CV but a law degree. And with a stream of other law graduates, I kept knocking on doors that slammed in my face.'

'Try again,' she said.

'I've been three years out of it,' he seethed. 'I'm rusty. I don't have a family firm to give me a desk. The bastards won't let me in.'

'So don't complain about the bloody job you do have!'

Both were silenced. Maggie poured the hot water in the teapot and took two mugs off the draining board. She immediately felt guilty at her outburst. The long day, the extra weight, hormones. Something. David sat on a chair by the kitchen table grinding his fists together. The kitchen was just big enough for a small table with two chairs, apart from the kitchen paraphernalia. Not big enough for a rowing couple.

'I'm sorry,' she said, coming to him, standing knee to his knees. 'I shouldn't have said that.'

'No, you are right.' He looked up to her. 'You should have said it. We are here together, however we are. I couldn't get into a solicitor's office, though I tried my hardest.'

'I know you did, dearest.'

'So I'm to be the area manager of a chain of coffee shops.' He sighed. 'I never wanted it. But you're right. It's a job. But the thought of 25 years...'

'It doesn't have to be 25 years,' she said, coming down to his height. 'If you can manage a dozen coffee shops, or whatever number, you can manage other things.'

He nodded and took her hands. She kissed him on the nose, knowing he was saying goodbye to his dream of being a human rights lawyer. She had no right telling him off. He was in the process of becoming someone else – and the metamorphosis involved breaking off his wings.

'Do what you want,' she said, 'and I will go with you.'

He stood up. There were tears in his eyes.

'It's why I married you,' he said. 'I will be area manager, Maggie. Three weeks and I take over. And I will endeavour to do it well. Take their money, do it and then...' His hands flew wide, 'we'll see what opens up.'

'We can predict the past,' she exclaimed, wagging a finger, 'but not the future.'

'What book of maxims did you get that from?'

'My mum told me it.'

'It is of course true then,' he said, 'but like most things your mother says – no help.'

There was a rap on the flat door. And a call.

'Hello, it's me. Anne.'

She was invited in and given a cup of tea. She was dressed up, they noted, a short, sleeveless red dress, her face made up. She said she couldn't stay long as she was mid cooking, but had something important to tell them. They shifted to the sitting room, three was a crowd in the kitchen.

'You have us both agog,' said Maggie. 'Spill.'

Anne hesitated a second, then jumped in.

'Frank followed you to your school this morning.'

She told them that the builder was the source of information, and that Frank, on being asked about it, denied he was there.

Maggie and David looked at each other, jolted by the sizzle of threat.

'How sure are you of this?' said Maggie.

'He says he saw the orange car, that Aurora of his, can't miss it, and Frank himself, outside your school.'

'But Frank says he wasn't there?' asked David.

'Denies it completely,' said Anne.

'He would, wouldn't he?' said Maggie, 'whether he was there or not.'

'How reliable is the builder?'

'He doesn't drink,' says Anne. 'And he's quite sharp.'

'Let's suppose he's right,' said David, turning to his wife. 'Why would he follow you?'

'All connected to the fight last night,' she said. 'Planning some sort of vengeance.'

'But I hit him,' said David. 'Not you.'

'He gets at you by getting at Maggie,' said Anne.

Maggie shuddered and grimaced. 'Ooh, it's so creepy, being followed by that lowlife.'

'There can't be many reasons why,' said David, the ticking of his thoughts almost visible. 'Some attack, rape...'

'What! In my condition?'

'Murder,' went on David, 'or kidnapping...'

'Bloody hell!' exclaimed Maggie. 'I am victim number one in a horror movie.'

'Could just be to put the frighteners on,' said Anne.

'Very effectively,' said Maggie.

'But that only works,' said David, 'if you are aware he's doing it. You wouldn't know, without the builder.'

'He just happened to be taking his daughter to school, Maggie.'

'I might ask you who his daughter is, but some other time. I'm feeling a little overwhelmed.'

'I could go down and confront him,' said David thoughtfully. 'Right now.'

'But he'll deny it,' said Maggie. 'And then you'll hit him again.'

'Alright,' said David. 'Let's use our three heads on this.'

'I'm not against you using your fists, love.'

He ignored her. 'Suppose I go to the police in the morning. At least they'll have it on record. And after I've done it, we tell him we've informed the police that he followed you.'

'Maybe write him a note,' said Maggie, 'instead of face to face, and so avoid a punch-up.'

'Maybe. Anyway, cop shop tomorrow. I'll go into work a bit late.' He turned to Anne. 'Thanks for telling us, Anne. It's as well to know.'

'I couldn't leave it there. I had to tell you.'

'Thank you so much,' said Maggie, putting a hand on Anne's.

'And I must go. Cooking.'

'Someone coming?' said Maggie, noting again her dress and make up. Anne nodded. 'Someone nice?'

'I hope so.'

'Who?'

'Tell you tomorrow, if, you know...'

'Bet it's the builder.'

Anne blushed and looked down at her hands.

'Oh, I'm sorry, Anne. Don't mind me teasing. I'm sure he's a very nice man.'

'It's been a long time since I've met one.'

'Go and do your cooking,' said David. 'And we hope it all goes well.'

Maggie got up.

'Hang about, Anne. I've got a bottle of wine for you.'

Anne waved her hands vigorously. 'Strictly no booze.

He's a teetotaller.'

And she kissed Maggie on the cheek, then David. 'Must run, must.'

They called their best wishes and thank yous as she darted from the flat.

Chapter 24

Jack's legs were hollow, his stomach fluttering as he entered her flat. He'd brought a pot plant, some sort of flowering cactus that the florist told him should continue flowering until after Christmas. He didn't like cut flowers; they went off in a few days and stank. Reminded him of funerals. Seemed much better value to give something growing. In his other hand was a box of chocolates, his alternative to a bottle of booze, though you could hardly get high on an orange delight.

Except adrenaline had got him to that pitch already. His body was charged as she opened wide the door, in a vibrant red dress, lips the same colour, wearing a prim white apron. He stepped inside and kissed her on the cheek, aftershave merging with her rose aroma.

She took off her apron.

'Everything is simmering nicely. Let's sit down for a minute.'

He'd not seen her sitting room, just the nursery and the kitchen. It was fairly minimalist. A bookshelf; he'd have a look at the books, they always told you a lot about people. There was a hatch into the kitchen, both its pine doors wide open, a smallish, pale brown sofa and a single armchair to match. Two brightly coloured framed prints were on the walls. That one with all the blues and umbrellas he should probably know. Alison would.

The table was set out for two, side by side. In the centre was a blue glass vase with a very thick base holding a mixture of late blooms.

Awkwardly he handed over the chocolates and the potted plant.

'My contribution.'

'Oh, a winter flowering cactus,' she exclaimed. 'They last ages.' And added with a laugh as she put it on a shelf,

'Still be around when I'm dead.'

She settled on the sofa and invited him to sit by her. On the coffee table was a bottle of elderflower champagne and two wine glasses in a wooden tray, embossed with a map of France with cartoon French men and women doing Gallic things with wine and food.

'Drink?' she said, holding up the bottle, 'non-alcoholic, only the best.'

'Please,' he said, finding words difficult. That was why you drank. Or smoked a cigarette. They busied the hands, got the blood moving. Though his was moving, perhaps too quickly, and stumbling over itself.

He said, 'The rain's stopped at long last.'

'Oh, you were so wet today.'

She handed him a drink, the bubbles fizzing and popping above the surface of the liquid.

'I do like the smell of elderflower champagne, the way it tickles your nose,' she said. 'You can smell the flowers.'

Jack had done the Cook's Tour of non-alcoholic drinks in the last year. There weren't many he hadn't tried in his efforts to replace booze in various cultural encounters.

'It's one of my favourites,' he said. 'It has a sly flavour.'

There was a few seconds' silence as both sipped. Weather done, the drink remarked upon. A topic, a topic – my kingdom for a topic!

'Did you speak to the people upstairs?' he said, anxiously grasping a flying thought.

She nodded. 'About half an hour ago. And I'm so glad I did. David's going to go to the police in the morning, and will drop a note in to Frank saying he's done so.'

'He's a slimy git,' exclaimed Jack. 'Who would put a tack in a meatball?'

'Maggie's quite scared that he followed her,' she said. 'She didn't say so, but I could tell. Six months pregnant on top of everything.'

'His daughter's terrified of him, you know,' said Jack.

'She did an errand for me earlier, and was frightened out of her wits when I told her her father was back and asking for her.'

'He beats her,' said Anne. 'And I suspect incest.'

'How do you know?'

Anne shrugged. 'A feeling. The way she is around him, his nastiness to her. The way he keeps her to him. She never goes anywhere apart from the shops. No friends I've seen.'

'Shouldn't it be reported?'

'Who to?' she said, 'and without Bessie getting a battering?'

'My ex would know, but I'm not about to ask her. Some women's organisation. I'm not up on this.'

'I should be,' said Anne. 'With the childminding course I did, we covered abuse. Kids, but it's not that different. I'll find out.'

'We can't leave her to him.'

'No. You're right. Tomorrow I'll chase it up. Find out who to contact. It's so difficult when it's neighbours, but we can't leave it. Now let's eat.'

They went to the table. He sat down. She took two square, green candles off a shelf and lit them. Then placed one on either side of the central vase in a flat dish. She turned down the room lights with the dimmer switch, which enhanced the candlelight, filling the room with flickering shadow.

Their meal began with a pinkish half melon each, with various fruits where the seeds had been scooped out: purple and green grapes, slices of kiwi fruit and satsuma segments.

'You've an eye for colour,' he said.

'Thank you,' she said, obviously pleased. 'I am sure if food looks good then it will more likely taste good.'

'I'm getting my five-a-day in one.'

'Tell me about your daughter.'

'Mia, she's ten,' he said. 'And I have the feeling, from

what she's said, Maggie might be her teacher. Mia said she was pregnant. Her mum's English co-ordinator there.'

'Small world.'

'Me and her mum have an uneasy relationship, let's say. But I get on well with Mia, mostly. We went out with the telescope last night. She knows the craters on the moon, and says she'd like to be an astronaut. We didn't get back till ten. That would have had her mum dancing on hot coals. But straight to bed, and she was fine in the morning.'

'I've two older children come to me after school,' said Anne, 'just for an hour or two, till their parents come back from work.'

'If you don't mind me saying...'

'I don't know whether I mind or not, till you say it.'

'You seem rather young for a childminder, and...' he hesitated, then continued regardless. 'I took a glance at your books. I think you're a graduate...'

She nodded. 'I did English and History at York.'

'And now you're a childminder.'

She gathered his bowl in which lay the melon rind, and with her own put it on the shelf of the hatch.

She said, 'I think you've sussed me.'

'I haven't sussed very much,' he said, somewhat puzzled.

'Well, before you start Googling me, I'd best tell you. Though let's have our main course first.'

She left the room and went into the kitchen via the hallway, where he watched her through the hatch. Some mystery about to be revealed. Did he want to know? Why not just a pleasant meal with candles and flowers, all dressed up, best behaviour – and no history of sins. Just romance. Talk only about films and fluff. Go out and look at the moon.

Keep secrets secret.

Anne opened the oven and a hot smell of mozzarella, tomato and spices filled the air. His stomach turned over; it was a long time since lunch and he'd not had time to eat anything. What with sorting out the fencing, then back to finish off the wall. As soon as that was done, he'd scooted home to clean up for tonight, squeezing in time to buy the pot plant and chocolates.

She had taken the used bowls off the hatch shelf, and placed on it the lasagne and salad, along with various serving utensils. Then Anne returned to the sitting room and placed the food on the table. With a slice, she served him a generous piece of lasagne.

'Plenty more if you want it,' she said. 'Help yourself to salad.'

'This is magnificent,' he said looking at his steaming plate. 'Much better than the chicken take-out I'd probably have.'

'Much better,' she said primly, and sat herself down.

He waited for her to begin the big topic. Didn't feel he should remind her, instead said complimentary things about the food. Not that it wasn't true. Much better than his usual fare. Though he tended to do better when Mia was round. She would complain if he didn't, besides which he owed it to her.

Anne said, 'I was about to answer your query...'

'You don't have to,' he said.

She screwed up her nose. 'I do. Besides, it's not something I should be ashamed of. Though I am still. But my counsellor said talk about it, don't make it a big secret.'

He took some salad, colourful with tomatoes, peppers, olives, and various hues of lettuce leaves. It had no dressing on. There was a little jug of it with a tiny spoon. He picked it up tentatively and sniffed.

'It's only lemon juice and olive oil,' she said.

He spooned a little on.

'I couldn't get a job,' she said, 'because I'd been in prison...'

'What for?' he said, taking care not to catch her eye, in his surprise at the sudden revelation.

She took a deep breath, gave a wry smile and said, 'For murdering my husband, Malcolm.'

Jack stopped chewing, his knife and fork held frozen as if he were the subject of a Victorian photograph.

'I didn't do it,' she said, closing her eyes for a second. 'The actual perpetrator fitted me up nicely,' she added with a short laugh. 'The CPS had a tight case, circumstantial. And lies from a couple of witnesses. Well, I was having an affair to make it worse. The upshot was I was found guilty. And spent two years in the nick. Horrible, horrible time. Then they found out who actually did it. And I was freed.'

'How long ago was this?'

'I've been out for three years,' she said. 'Once I was free, I got Malcolm's life insurance and the money for his flat. I didn't want to stick around in Manchester. Too many people had said nasty things about me. I wanted a fresh start. So came down to London. Bought this flat and spent a year trying to get a job. It does make a mess of a CV, two years in jail. Even telling lies about it means you have to tell more to fill in what you were doing in the time. In the end I thought, I have a bit of money, what can I do? And came up with childminding. I did a course, got the nursery set up, went through the inspection...' She bit her thumb. 'I was so thoroughly inspected. That prison spell stumped them for a bit, till I went to a solicitor, and they caved in. Got my first children six months ago. And here I am. Ex jailbird makes good.'

'That's quite a story,' said Jack, busying himself eating, while he worked out how to respond.

'Bit of a show stopper,' she said. 'But my counsellor was right. The more I tell it, the less guilty I feel. OK, I was having an affair, but that's not the same as murder... Though to read the tabloids you might think so. If you're curious, you'll find it all online, in various versions.' She stood up, waved her hands as if to flap all her past away. 'Let's have some music, and some lighter talk to drive out my lurid tale and thoughts of him upstairs.'

She went to the music unit and began sorting through CDs.

Jack's phone rang.

Annoyed, knowing he should have turned it off, he took it out of his pocket and looked to see who was interrupting his dinner date.

Alison.

'Do you mind?' he said, holding up his ringing phone.

'Go ahead,' she said.

He stepped out into the hall.

'I hope this is important, Alison. I'm in the middle of eating.'

'Mia has run off.'

'What do you mean run off?'

'I told her I'd got the Brighton job. She got sulky. So I sent her to her room. Next thing I know, the front door slams and I see her going off in a car...'

'A taxi?'

'I suspect so. Has she come to you?'

'I'm not at home.'

'Well, she's not answering my calls. Will you phone her and get back to me?'

'Right. Let me try. I'll phone you straight back after I've spoken to her.'

He rang off. And his phone rang almost instantly. It was Mia.

'Where are you?' he said.

'At your place, Dad. Outside your front door. It's cold.'

'Stay there. I'll be right along.'

'I've been ringing and ringing. Where are you?'

'Tell you when I see you. I'll be there, say fifteen minutes.'

With goodbyes on either side, he rang off. There was no point cross examining her on the phone. Get to her first.

Details later. He went back into the sitting room. And told Anne about the family crisis.

'Sorry, Anne, but I've got to go and get her. Right away.'

'You must,' said Anne.

'I'll sort it out quick as I can. And then come back, if you'll have me.'

'Be off,' she said. 'And please come back. Take my spare front door key.'

He took the key, assuming it meant he could come back very late if needs be, so things were not bad here at all. Just Mia and her mother to sort out. He kissed Anne on the cheek, then the lips. A long embrace. And then, with the greatest reluctance, he pulled away.

'Save some pudding for me, Anne.'

And shot away.

PART TWO:
THE FIRST KILLING

Chapter 25

Mia was a bundle in the doorway, pathetic and cold, like a homeless waif. By her side a small suitcase with the few precious items she'd chosen to run away with. He helped her get up, kissed her on the forehead and took her suitcase. Jack opened the door and ushered her into the hallway.

They went upstairs to the flat. And immediately Jack turned on the gas fire. He sat Mia in an armchair, put a blanket over her knees, and went into the kitchen to make hot chocolate. There, he phoned Alison. And told her Mia was here. Alison said she'd be over right away.

He kept up an inane commentary from the kitchen to show he was there and doing things: 'Kettle on, chocolate going in the cups, adding milk, milk back in the fridge, adding sugar, although it's not good for you...'

'I know how to make hot chocolate, Dad,' she called back.

'Tell me soon as I go wrong then. Kettle off, pour water on the floor...'

'Wrong.'

'Just testing. I'm sure it's a lot better in the cup. Stir, stir more. Spoon in the sink.'

He took the two hot chocolates into the sitting room, not really wanting one himself, but thought it more companionable to have one. He handed her a cup. And noted that, warm again, she was coming back to life.

'Your mum's coming over,' he said. 'You'd better fill me in.'

She screwed up her nose. 'I don't want to go to Brighton.'

'Your mum's not going to take you to Brighton tomorrow. It's not for...' he calculated, 'two and a half months.'

'I want to go to Atwoods with my friends.'

'You haven't been accepted at Atwoods yet. Neither have your friends.'

She shrugged. 'We will be.'

'Maybe you will, maybe you won't.'

She ignored the uncertainty and said, 'She just sprung it on me. We're going to Brighton, she said. 'We' – like I'm a dog on a lead.'

'It's promotion for your mum,' he said, trying hard. 'Deputy head, you know. Extra pay. You'll find somewhere better to live, not far from the sea. Brighton's got a lot of life.'

'Can't I stay with you in London?'

He blew out his cheeks. 'And how would that work, you over here in Forest Gate? You'd have an hour's journey every day to Atwoods in Hackney. If they accept you. This place is alright if you stay the odd weekend. But you haven't even got your own room. Alright if you've not much here, but you would if you lived here as your main home. Besides, your mum will be earning nearly twice what I make.'

'Money isn't everything.'

He couldn't help a laugh. Wisdom from the ten year old perspective.

'It's not everything, I admit,' he said, 'but a decent, regular income doesn't half make life easier.'

There was a ring on the bell.

'Your mum. I'd best let her in.'

He left the flat, went down the stairs and opened the front door. There was Alison, flustered with speed and worry.

'How is she?'

'Fine.'

'What have you been saying to her?'

'That Brighton is a nice place and you earn nearly twice what I do.'

She punched him on the shoulder.

'Thanks, Jack.'

'You are ruining my dinner date,' he said as she came in and followed him up the stairs.

'Are you on a promise?' she said.

'Was. Might yet be. If I can get back there.'

'I do appreciate this, Jack. And will do my best to get you back.'

They went in the flat.

'Hello, Mum,' said Mia.

She was seated with the blanket over her knees like a recovered invalid, a book on her lap. Jack noted it was an Enid Blyton. If Alison did, she didn't say anything.

'I'll make you some tea, Alison,' said Jack.

He went in the kitchen. Let them get talking. He'd said his piece and didn't want to compete with Alison. And as much as he wanted to get back to Anne, he knew this couldn't be hurried. In this muddled family were three relationships, each dependent on the others. And for himself, he'd rather Alison didn't go to Brighton. Or rather he didn't want Alison and Mia going to Brighton. But how could he complain with his insecure income? She'd been offered a good job, quite a bit more money, and Brighton was an exciting town. Not a bad time for Mia to move either. She'd only have to do two terms in primary before she went to secondary school. Except she wanted to go to Atwoods with her mates.

He took a tea in to Alison, amid her apology to Mia for her hastiness. And for putting it to her so bluntly, and not explaining herself properly. And then there was out and out bribery. A laptop. Jack gasped at this. Not sure if you should do such things. Didn't they rebound on you, come to be expected?

Perhaps every time you moved to Brighton, so maybe not so bad. And then somehow he was roped in. And the three of them arranged to go to Brighton the coming weekend.

'Not in your van,' said Alison. 'It's always full of your stuff and not suitable for a long journey.'

The alternative was her car, he thought, or...

'Let's go by train,' he said. 'It's only an hour or so from London Bridge or Victoria.'

'Yes, by train,' said Mia.

And that settled it. Train times would be settled on later in the week, but all three would have a day at the seaside on Saturday. Crisis over. A laptop and a day at the seaside. He'd have to be on best behaviour to spend a day with Alison.

Deal done, Alison got Mia on the move.

As they were leaving the flat, he heard Mia say:

'Maybe not a laptop. For the same money, I could get a pretty good Dobsonian telescope... And if we get a garden in a darker part of town...'

He felt quite jealous for an instant, having to drive out of town to set up his telescope. But then thought, Anne has an OK garden, if that relationship goes anywhere, if it should last...

If it should start.

He looked out of the window to make sure Mia and Alison were safely away. Then headed off to get his pudding.

Chapter 26

Frank was on his way back from the pub, staggering somewhat. It was a chilly night, the sky quite clear with a three-quarter moon rising. His jacket was open, he was not feeling the cold, the alcohol desensitising him in his slow stroll. A bacon roll when he got back, get her lazy self on it.

He'd met a few regulars in the Goose, had a josh with them over his black eye and loose tooth, and mulled over his own ideas on the walk back. He was strict about drinking and driving. He was a cab man, known for that, and if caught over the limit he'd lose his driving licence and his livelihood. Drink, sure, it was an Englishman's right, but walk home, though he was sure he could drive, but you can't argue with a copper holding a breathalyser. A few pints always sharpened his wits, but no way was he going to risk it. Why, a couple of weeks ago, he'd even got a cab home!

Tonight was a moderate night drinkwise. Frank'd had a few, say three or four, five at the very outside. Who was counting? Bert wasn't there. Pity, as he liked to swap sentiments with him; they agreed on the state of the nation, about the role of women and what they were good for. Always great for a laugh and a challenge was Bert. Coming over tomorrow anyway, bringing a couple of steaks. He salivated at the thought of a rare steak, the blood coming through the flesh. He'd get Bessie on that. And she'd better get it right or he'd teach her. Then while the men ate, send her out, and the two of 'em could plan what to do with the mongrel couple.

He had some thoughts of his own. For instance, Bert had a white van, used for his family butcher's shop. But good for other things. All they had to do was get the lady in, somehow, and it was all up for grabs.

Bert's place, up Epping, might figure in the scenario. A quaint workingman's cottage, all on its own, surrounded by forest. But it had to be a clean pick up, no one seeing them. Or rule it out. And assuming that, then he'd give her one, show her what a white man could do, for comparison's sake. They had balaclavas, which meant she'd have no idea who they were, and once done with her, could pitch her out in the forest somewhere. Naked. That appealed. Likely Bert would have some suggestions of his own.

A rare steak with onions, spuds and mushrooms, a few beers – and they could plan a creative bit of villainy.

Their light was on at the top of the house, he noted. Was the darkie banging her one right now? Never stop, these niggers. She had his brown bun in the oven already. And still he'd be on top of her. He'd listened in the night to their bed springs. Sickening. He spat on to the pavement, a hand on the outside wall to steady himself.

Nancy was in too, but his own flat light was off. Bessie must be with that silly old cow. Time he put a stop to that. It'd just give her cat fleas. That was, if the cat survived its picky meal.

Smart idea, mince and tacks. The stupid moggie would choke like it had a steel fishbone stuck in its gullet. Or so went the theory. If it worked, all to the good, if not modify. He was quite scientific in his plans.

She was in too, her downstairs. Lot of rounded flesh there, in all the right places. He rubbed his groin. Lived by herself, not seen any other guys coming and going. Must be dying for it. Time he paid her a visit, being neighbours. Things to discuss, points to be made before someone else made them.

Frank's fingers fumbled to get the key in the lock. Wrong bloody key, they all looked the same in this light. He tried again and opened the front door. Why not a visit? She was up, probably just watching TV. He'd be busy tomorrow night. Seize the day, as they say.

He walked up the hallway to Anne's door. Straightened himself up, be confident and forceful, that was the way. He rapped sharply on the door with his knuckles like he knew he'd be welcome. And why shouldn't he be? Inside, music was playing. Jazz or something. He could turn that up a bit as things got moving.

The door opened.

'You're back quick... Oh, it's you.'

Before she could react further, he pushed past her into the flat.

'I'd like to talk to you about the lease, Anne.'

Chapter 27

Bessie and Nancy were at the end of the flowerbed, almost in darkness, well back from the house where the hall light was on. Tickles was wandering about somewhere, and Nancy, sitting in an aluminium folding chair, was watching, the rusty biscuit box in her lap.

Bessie was digging a hole with her trowel. The ground was soft after the rain. She had chosen a bit of her flowerbed, not the wall side, well, where the wall had been. It was all gone now, awaiting the fence. There was a bright moon, not full but going that way. Full would have been better, but tonight he was out at the pub and she had to make the best of the chance. She had her coat on, buttoned up, to keep out the chill.

'It's cold,' shivered Nancy. 'I want to get back to my bed.'

'Won't be long,' said Bessie. 'The box was under his bed all last night, absorbing the essence of him. It's packed full of his aura.' She continued digging, a mound of soil building up beside her. 'We're nearly finished. We must call on the spirits who fly by moonlight. And then bury the box in the earth.'

'I'm not sure I like this sort of thing,' said Nancy, bending and unbending her arthritic fingers. They were stiffening in the chill. 'Where's Tickles?' She looked about her in the shadowy darkness.

'Don't worry. I won't leave him out,' said Bessie.

She was a little on edge herself. Her father could come back anytime. He'd beat her if she wasn't there. She'd have to risk that. In fact, all the more reason to. She was here for all the years of beatings, for every time he'd had her. She looked up at the moon, hoping the spirits were flying tonight. You couldn't see them, unless you had the eye – and she didn't.

She stuck the trowel in the soil and rubbed her hands together to wipe the earth off her fingers. If this didn't work, then she would have to kill him herself. She'd thought about it many nights, lying there beside him. Him snoring away, she lying so close. All she needed was the kitchen knife.

But the magic would work. The website said so. Done with care and belief. You had to believe, and not rush the forces. Believing was the impetus.

'And now we call on the spirits,' said Bessie. 'Give me the box.'

Nancy handed her the biscuit box. And Bessie put it in the hole she had dug. It rested three or four inches below ground level. She took a crumpled piece of paper from her pocket and gave it to Nancy. 'You must read the words slowly, I will repeat each line after you, and will throw earth in the hole.'

Nancy fumbled to put on her glasses, her fingers thick in the cold. The glasses were opaque with condensation. She had to remove them and wipe them on her sleeve. And fumblingly, put them back on again.

'I can't read it,' she exclaimed, moving the paper back and forth. 'It's too dark.'

Bessie was prepared for this and took a little torch from her pocket and switched it on. She handed it to Nancy.

'Just point it downwards,' said Bessie. 'Coat round, so we can't be seen from the house. The main light must be from the moon.'

She looked upwards. The moon was free of cloud, glowing golden with smudges on its surface like dirty fingerprints on a plate.

'That's better,' said Nancy as the words came into her vision. She twisted her body round to shield the light, both hands occupied holding the paper and torch. 'That's the best I can do.'

'Read,' said Bessie, trowel in hand. 'Slowly. Line by line.'

Nancy began reading, the torch playing over the paper. Bessie repeated each line after her, throwing soil into the hole with her trowel, as if it were a burial.

I summon up thee, great Beelzebub,
Enjoin these believers to thy hub.
I summon up thee, mighty Hecate,
Thou who knows what this curse may be;
Let the soul of Frank Brand be revoked.
Evil ones, thy magic is evoked,
May he die this night in agony,
And we will forever worship thee.

The spell completed, in silence Bessie continued filling the hole.

Chapter 28

Jack put on his safety belt and set off for Anne's, with some relief after all his rushing about. Crisis resolved. He'd sped home to get Mia, placated her, and with Alison got her half agreeing to move to Brighton. With the aid of a big bribe. Still, a move was a cosmic event in a kid's life, torn away from friends and the future she saw herself in. With no say in the matter.

But then you can't negotiate a career move to Brighton with a child. Well you could, but then the child controlled your life. Anyway, child placated, Alison happy, move on – and hope that he had a life beyond fatherhood.

The traffic was light. The only tricky bit was crossing the Romford Road. He never trusted drivers this time of night. Too many still drank, in spite of the drink driving laws. He'd done so himself, and almost killed himself. There should be a gadget in the car, which if it detected any booze fumes, wouldn't let the car start.

He'd have to invent it.

Anyway, all set for a family visit to Brighton on Saturday. The sea and rock and a kiss-me-quick hat. He always enjoyed the seaside, watching the waves coming in forever. He hoped it would be a good day out. And not all blow up into a family row.

Though he and Alison had got on OK tonight. Parents United. No recriminations from her, no sarky remarks. Maybe they'd turned a corner. He was no longer her drunken ex. There was obvious sense in being friends; they had part-share in Mia's upbringing for the next ten years or so. Sparring parents would do her no good at all.

And now, could he rescue the rest of his evening?

Back on Ham Park Road, Jack got out of the van and locked up. He was parked just behind the orange Aurora. Frank's vehicle. Quite a smart little car he had. Though it was his job, so he had to look after it. He was, though, a slimeball. Condemned as a parent and as a neighbour. What had happened in his life to make him so vile?

He must remind Anne about doing something about Bessie. Contacting the right people.

But that was tomorrow. Tonight, what was left of it, had to be put straight. He had his own life. One step at a time. She might just be too tired, gone off the boil, so to speak. Well, see if he was welcomed back. They'd been getting on fine, he and Anne, then the phone call. A missive from another world. And he was transformed, in an instant, from lover to parent. Well, the parent was back in the box, the lid shut down tight.

The lover pads the street.

Her light was on. In fact, it was the only one on in the house, apart from the hall light. He searched about in his pocket for the front door key she'd loaned him. Found it and opened the front door. This was déjà vu. He needed the chocolates and pot plant to present to her for the rewind. And felt as nervous as he had at the beginning of the evening. More so.

He stood at her door. Combed his hair, straightened his collar, might've showered and shampooed if they'd been available, brushed his shoes behind his shins, looked at his nails. He knew it made no difference; it was simply prevarication.

He could just go home, of course. And in the morning make up some excuse, exaggerate the family crisis. But he wasn't going home, he knew. Unless she slammed the door in his face. He took a step back against the hall wall. Pressed against it with his hands, took a big breath, and stepped forward resolutely and rapped on the door.

There. Done. All set for his apologies. He could hear

footsteps. His hands slipped against his thighs. His fingers crossed and uncrossed – as the door opened.

Anne was there, her face smeared with blood.

It took him a few seconds to take her in. She was in her red dress, though it was ripped at the cleavage, and both cheeks and forehead were blood splattered, as was her neck. Hands too.

Gripping the door as if it were all that held her up, she said, 'I've killed him, Jack.'

'Who?'

'Frank.'

He didn't move. No longer eager to cross the threshold into her arms.

'Do you want to come in?' she said.

He thought rapidly. What was she inviting him into? He could just leave, be no part of whatever she'd done. Let her sort it out. Except he was here. Already too late. He was involved. A witness to whatever. There was no simply going away. He was involved the instant the door opened.

'He tried to rape me,' she said.

'Fuck,' he said.

An expression of helplessness, confusion and weakness. She turned about and went into the flat. He, no longer caring about the condition of his hair or nails, followed her, closing the door behind him, breathing heavily with expectation.

She led him into the sitting room.

On the sofa lay Frank. His head was smashed in, blood congealing on his face, one arm hung languidly down the sofa. About him were scattered flowers and blue glass fragments. A large solid fragment, the base of the vase with shards, as if growing from it, lay near his head. His shirt was splashed in blood and water.

'He pushed his way in,' she said, 'pretty drunk. I thought it was you when he knocked. Said he wanted to talk about the lease, white people together. Though pretty obviously, he hadn't much interest in the lease – and came on to me.

He got very forceful all at once, was tearing my dress off though I was yelling for him to stop. He slapped me and punched me...' She stopped, deflated by the memory. After a pause, she swallowed and added, 'So I grabbed what I could – and smashed him on the head with it.' She indicated the body and mess on the sofa. 'With that result. About fifteen minutes ago.'

He was gazing at the tableau, noting among the glass and blood, Frank's belt was undone, the top buttons of his fly free.

'What have you been doing since...' his hand flapped at the sofa, 'that?'

'Sitting here. Waiting for you.'

He was bludgeoned. Couldn't take his eyes off the sofa. A bleeding corpse with flowers and glass. Reason swept away in the tsunami of shock.

'Do you want a coffee?' she said.

He numbly nodded.

She went out and into her kitchen. He followed like an automaton.

She put the kettle on. He closed the shutters of the hatch. The sitting room no longer existed. He was shivering. Things had to be done. He couldn't fool himself. The sitting room did exist and there was a body in it. A man who had been murdered, or was it manslaughter or was it some other crime, he couldn't think what. A man, though, with his head smashed in. And one was supposed to do something, as a respectable citizen.

'The last thing I expected,' he said emptily.

'You came back for pudding,' she said. 'I've kept some for you.'

'You've killed him,' he said.

'He was raping me. I grabbed what I could in panic. And smashed his head in. He stopped at once.'

Jack sank onto a stool, engulfed in weariness. He remembered what Alison had said maybe an hour ago. 'Are you on a promise?' Oh yes, a promise, he was on that alright.

She was making the coffee. Instant, stirring the cups, adding milk. Stirring again.

'We should call the police,' he said.

She handed him a coffee.

'No.'

'No?' he queried. 'Not call the police?'

She said, 'Five years ago, I found my husband dead when I came home. I called the police that time. And I was arrested for his murder. And served two years.'

'You told me.'

'So you know why I'm not going through that again.'

He took a sip of coffee. This was limbo. Before life changed irrevocably. He knew what she was going to say, but pressed her to say it.

'What's the alternative?'

She was seated on a stool. Their knees were nearly touching. A few hours ago, he'd have found that arousing. Her slim legs, short, sleeveless dress, ripped at the cleavage. But blood spattered, she might have been a flank of beef.

She said, 'There's only one alternative.'

He was overwhelmed by all that entailed. The body had to be removed. Dumped somewhere, anywhere. Just not here.

She said, 'I was hoping you'd help me.'

Here was the Rubicon, he had a foot on the bridge. He could turn about. And go home, or phone the police. But he'd kissed her, she'd made him a meal. She'd invited him in from the rain. He was on a promise.

He said, 'We could dump him in the canal.'

She nodded vigorously. Took his hands. 'Please.'

Suddenly he was charged with energy. St George with a maiden to rescue.

'I've got a large builder's bag in my van,' he said. 'We put him in that. Take him to the canal. And drop him in.'

'Yes, yes,' she said eagerly. 'Let's do it, Jack.'

He went out to his van to get the bag.

Chapter 29

They began at the feet. Taking Frank's shoes off to make it easier to get him in. His feet were smelly, the socks worn for some days. And then, bit by bit, they dragged the large bag underneath and over the cab driver. Once the legs were in, Jack had to lift the buttocks while Anne pulled the bag under. He lifted Frank's back up to the seated position and held him, almost like a ventriloquist, and they drew the bag up as if it were a sleeping bag. His head sagged, leaning on a shoulder, lips parted, tongue hanging out. The neck of the bag reached his nose and would go no further.

They began again at his feet, and as if drawing on a pair of tights, eased more bag under the corpse, dragging out the wrinkles, moving them forward, under his legs and buttocks, moving them up the prone and heavy body. Until there was sufficient slack to cover his head.

Anne put his shoes inside the bag.

'His pockets,' said Jack. 'We should empty them.'

'Does it matter?'

'I don't know. But let's do it, in case.'

He hardly knew of what, vaguely thinking of the discovering of the body, delaying identification.

To get to his pockets, they had to draw the bag back down his body, like a film reversed, under his neck and back, and down again to his buttocks. Until his trouser pockets were revealed.

Anne took out car keys, some change, a dirty handkerchief, some screwed up receipts, a betting slip.

'What do we do with them?' she said.

'Don't put anything in the bag that could help identify

him,' he said, thinking of the cop shows and CSI programmes on TV.

'I'll look in his jacket,' she said.

It was on the floor, crumpled at the foot of the sofa where he'd dropped it. She picked it up and went through the pockets. A phone, a wallet – she hastily looked through, some money, credit cards, odd bits of paper.

'Leave it all on the table,' he said. 'We'll sort it out later. Let's dump this body first.'

A pool of his pocket items was left on the table. They turned back to Frank, who was encased in milky plastic, slightly blurry like a fish under the ice.

'We need to seal the bag,' said Anne.

Jack put the jacket in the bag, pushing it well down, while Anne took some string and scissors out of a drawer. She brought them over and tied the neck of the bag, going round and round many times then tying excessive knots.

They stood, looking at each other, undecided what to do next. The body was in a bag. The easy bit done. And then? It had to be taken away, Jack knew.

'Before we go out,' said Jack, 'you'd better wash and change. You look like a butcher.'

She left him.

Jack looked about the room, considering what had to be done. The bag had to be taken out of the flat and put in his van. And then driven off and dumped wherever. But the first step was, get it out of this room. He began making space to drag it, moving the coffee table and armchair aside. He needed a clear run to the door.

That done, he rolled Frank off the sofa and onto the carpet. He took the legs and tried pulling but his hands kept slipping off the plastic with little forward motion. Frank would have to be rolled.

Fingerprints, he suddenly thought. All over the bag. His. They'd have to wipe it before dropping the bag in the canal. One thing at a time. Get him there first.

The furniture had to be moved still further back to make room for a rolling body. Then he began the roll. It worked, after a fashion. Though it was more a lift and drop than a roll. He traversed the body over the carpet, stopped at the door. He wiped his brow with the back of his hand, this was hard work. Next problem was how to get through the short section of hallway to the front door of Anne's flat. Too narrow to be rolled.

This was Jack in work mode. A problem to be solved. In this instance, an inanimate, slippery lump to be moved from A to B. What would a builder do?

It would have to be pulled, but not on the slippery plastic. He took the scissors and cut a line in the plastic by Frank's feet. Then putting his hands through the plastic, grasped Frank round his ankles, and pulled the corpse out of the sitting room door. As he'd hoped, the bag stayed on the body. And he drew the corpse along the hallway to the flat door.

Anne appeared. She was washed, and in jeans and an orange long sleeve top.

'Open the flat door,' he said.

She edged past the corpse, keeping to the wall, and opened the door. The light was on in the hall. He'd have preferred it off but better to see what they were doing and get the body out of the house quickly.

The bag and contents snagged on the raised wood at the door threshold, the legs and buttocks outside, head and torso in the flat.

'Can you get your hands underneath where it's sticking?' said Jack urgently. 'Give him a bit of a lift, so I can pull him through.'

Anne crouched in her flat hallway. She managed to get her hands partially underneath, but was shoved into a corner and the body couldn't get past her. The more Jack pulled, the more he pulled the body over her, as if Frank was trying again to rape her through the plastic.

'Stop, Jack! It's stuck on me,' she cried, pushing at one of Frank's arms.

'Shh!' hissed Jack. 'You'll wake the house.'

He stopped pulling, and lifted the body off Anne. She shuddered and rose. And came out into the hallway. There she leaned against the wall, catching her breath. The body was still half out of the flat, bent into an L-shape.

'Are you alright?' said Jack.

'OK now,' she nodded. 'Let's get it out and away. I can do more from out here.'

She got down on her knees and put her hands under the centre of the body. 'There, he's lifting. Pull now.'

They were interrupted by a yelling from the back door, heading their way. Bessie was running in full panic, Tickles in her arms, the cat gurgling and frothy, legs and paws outstretched.

She saw Jack and screamed.

'Save him! Save him!'

Her face was dirt covered, smeared in tears. She stood before him with her offering. Nancy was padding down the hallway, her stick clomping the floor.

Jack stood helplessly by the bagged corpse, the legs and buttocks in the hallway, one glance in the flat would reveal the rest.

Except Bessie was only interested in the choking cat in her arms. Jack at once understood the problem.

'Open its jaws,' he said. 'Wide as you can.' When she hesitated, he ordered, 'Do it.'

She lifted the jaws with the cat stretching and convulsing.

'More. Wide as you can,' exclaimed Jack.

'I'm hurting him,' squealed Bessie.

Anne came to help, yanking the jaws wide in spite of the thrashing cat. Jack put his fingers in the animal's throat. The cat was gurgling frantically, desperate to pull away. Jack pushed his fingers further in, grazing the razor edged teeth. And grasped it. With a tug, the obstruction came out. A long tack.

He held it up for the others to see.

'Thank you, thank you!' exclaimed Bessie. She stroked Tickles. 'Oh, you poor thing. He'll be alright now.'

She put down the cat, who circled his head round and round, spat and hissed. And walked over to Nancy. And rubbed his back against her leg as if to say here was one at least who wouldn't force open his jaws and put fingers down his throat.

Bessie threw her arms round Jack's waist. 'I'll be your friend forever.'

Anne was holding the tack.

'What's going on down there?' came a call from above.

They all looked up. There were David and Maggie in their dressing gowns, leaning on the banisters.

'It's alright, it's nothing,' Anne called up. 'Emergency over.'

Bessie saw the bag at the flat door. Jack saw her looking and waited for her reaction. Tickles was licking the bag end where Jack had cut the hole and a little blood had collected.

'It's him!' she yelled. 'Nancy, it worked! I told you. Look, there. It worked!'

She was dancing about and pointing. Jack was frantic to hush her, but it was all too late. David and Maggie were coming down the stairs. Anne there, Jack, Bessie and Nancy all staring at the bag and its contents.

'It's Frank,' said David, turning to his wife. 'All bagged up.'

'What's he doing in there?' said Maggie stupidly, peering in disbelief, half asleep.

Jack and Anne looked at each other. Jack blew out his cheeks, Anne threw out her arms in dumbshow.

Jack said, 'He's dead.'

That was obvious enough, but the obvious often needs to be stated.

'I killed him,' exclaimed Bessie, biting her lip.

Anne and Jack looked at her in puzzlement.

'He deserves everything he's got,' declared Nancy.

'I'm in the dark,' said Maggie, pulling her gown round herself. 'All I know is Frank is dead and in a plastic bag. Would someone care to explain?'

Anne said, 'Let's go inside. And I'll give chapter and verse.'

Chapter 30

They assembled in the nursery, the sitting room being unfit for company. A chair was found for Nancy and for Maggie, the others sat on the floor in the story area, making the best of the carpet and cushions. At the back was a low shelf of children's picture books. Jack left Anne to explain while he made coffee.

'I did it,' said Bessie for the umpteenth time.

Anne sighed and said, 'You did not, Bessie. I hit him with a vase. He was trying to rape me.'

'On my calling,' said Bessie, ambiguously. She would not be trumped.

'Congratulations,' said David to Anne.

'Three cheers,' said Nancy.

Anne had her arms round her knees, she was looking at the carpet a few feet in front of her. 'It was self preservation. I lashed out with the vase to get him off me. And that was that.'

'You don't need to convince me,' said Maggie. 'That vermin was capable of anything. I'm sure it was self defence. But I don't understand what the body is doing in a plastic bag in the hall...'

'Work it out,' said David with a yawn.

'Give me your managerial expertise,' she said.

'They're removing the body.'

'I got that far,' said Maggie. 'It's the why of it I don't get.'

'Why I haven't called the police?' said Anne helpfully.

'In a nutshell, yes. You didn't murder him. It's what's called – manslaughter, self defence or something.'

'It's called whatever they choose to call it,' said Anne.

Jack came in with the coffees on a tray. He placed it on the carpet and handed the mugs round.

Anne said, 'I have an aversion to cops.'

'Explain,' said David.

And she told her tale. Tickles was sitting on the rug and purring while Bessie stroked his back. It was story time. It might have been three year olds listening to *The Tiger Who Came To Tea*, but with coffee instead of juice. Jack crept off and got biscuits, feeling very much part of the hosting team. Chocolate fingers, part of the leftovers from dinner.

'OK,' said Maggie, when Anne had told her tale, 'It's clear why you don't like cops.'

Her feet were bare and she was massaging one in her lap.

'Do you want a blanket?' said Anne. 'And you,' she added to Nancy whose hands were going blue.

'I'm alright...' began Maggie, but Anne was already up and crossing the room.

'There's a body in the hallway,' said David, thinking aloud.

'I did it,' said Bessie. 'I called for his death.'

'Why did you?' said David to Bessie, putting up a hand to stop others intervening.

'Because of what he did to me,' she said.

She picked up Tickles and held him to her.

'What did he do to you?' said David.

'Nasty things.'

She said no more, intent on stroking Tickles. David didn't press it. They all knew of the beatings, and might surmise the nasty things. Anne returned with two blankets. She gave one to Maggie and helped Nancy spread it over her knees and legs.

'Thank you, dear.'

'Does anyone want to speak up for the bastard?' said David.

'He was a thorough going rotter,' exclaimed Nancy.

'He put tacks in meatballs to get your cat,' said Jack.

'I'd have killed him!' cried Nancy, 'if you hadn't.'

'He won't be missed,' said Maggie, looking like a passenger on a boat deck with the blanket over her knees.

Anne was back in the story seat, her legs bent under her.

She said, 'It's all up to you now, what to be done. He's lying in the hallway, awaiting your decision.'

'We either call the police or take him somewhere else,' said Maggie.

'Yes,' said Jack. 'One or the other.'

'Do any of you think the cops will believe me,' said Anne, 'in view of what happened last time?'

There was silence. The chocolate fingers were almost gone.

Bessie said, 'Get rid of the body.'

They looked to her, a little surprised at the vehemence.

'It wasn't her fault,' she said. 'I brought it on.'

This was not one to argue with. Not now.

'It'd be easy enough,' said David. 'Just take him to the forest and bury him.'

'I was thinking the canal,' said Jack.

David shook his head vehemently as if he were an expert on body disposal. 'He'll surface too quickly. Bury him in the forest, and he might never be found. Have we got any spades?'

'Two in the shed,' said Bessie.

'There you are,' said David. 'You game, Jack?'

'Yes.'

'Settled,' said David rising. 'Let's get on with it. Whose car?'

'I was thinking of my van...' began Jack.

Anne interrupted. 'No. Take his. We've got the keys.'

'Yes,' said Maggie excitedly, seeing a way of getting in on the game. 'I follow you in my car. You leave his in the forest, much better than outside here.'

They were all on their feet.

'You alright here?' said Jack to Anne.

'Yes, lots of cleaning up to do in the sitting room.' She turned to Bessie. 'Will you help me?'

'Of course I will,' she said. 'Let's scrub him away.'

Chapter 31

In the hallway, Maggie tied string round the head and feet of the parcelled corpse. At each end she bound the plastic bag with about a half-centimetre thick coil, then securely knotted the ends.

'Girl Guide stuff,' she said. 'You can lift it now with the string as handholds.'

Maggie went out in the street while David and Jack watched from the front door. There was a bright moon, lowering in the west of the sky. They had perhaps four hours of night. She opened the boot of the Aurora, and then stood on the street as lookout. There was little traffic and no pedestrians.

She nodded and raised a hand.

David and Jack picked up the body using the handholds. A good idea of Maggie's; the string cut into your fingers but the bundle was liftable. A glove would be better for a longer portage, Jack thought. He, being in front, had to walk backwards, out of the hallway and into the chilly night, slowly down the steps and onto the ceramic tiles of the path.

'Stop!' hissed Maggie.

They brought the body to the ground and ducked down. A car came past. They let it die away.

'OK,' called Maggie.

Jack and David picked up the body. They carried it through the open gate. This was the tricky part, on the pavement. If anyone were to come, there'd be no hiding place. Jack stumbled, backing over the kerb, and dropped his end.

'Fuck.'

He quickly picked the end up. And led David, with his

end, to the kerb and down carefully, until they were parallel to the boot of the car with their burden. The boot was empty, as a cab driver's needed to be for passengers' luggage. And so it was easy enough for them to lift the bag and contents over the lip and lay it inside. They shifted the load somewhat, bent the legs, then, satisfied, Jack was about to close the lid when Bessie ran out of the garden gate carrying two spades.

'Don't forget these!' she called.

'Good girl,' said Jack.

She beamed.

He put the spades in the boot. And slammed it shut.

'Let's go,' said David.

He had Frank's car door open. Jack could see from his stance he was not quite so confident under the night sky. This was no longer the jolly jape it seemed in the nursery.

Jack took the kerbside seat. Maggie was behind them in her car, waiting.

David drove off. Maggie waited a little before heading after. She was to keep some way back so it wouldn't look as if she were following them. The plan was to wait for her at any turn off.

'I've been walking in Epping Forest lots of times,' David said to Jack as he drove. 'I know a quiet car park. Be there in twenty minutes or so. Barring accidents.'

Jack was shaky. It was one thing being in Anne's flat, door shut, but now they were ferrying a corpse across town. One that had been murdered, or was it manslaughter, or however adjudged, they were accessories to some dark deed. He wondered whether David was regretting his involvement. It's a guy thing to say yes to the damsel in distress, but then, hey presto, you're in distress too. Anne was safe at home, and her two bit players driving with a hot corpse in the boot.

Explain that to a nosy cop.

Perverting the course of justice or something like that.

What might they get for that? A year, two years? Jack had little idea. And had no wish to find out.

Of course, they could turn back – and undo what they'd done. Put the corpse back in the sitting room, take it out of the bag and lay it out on the sofa, all ready for the police. But movement, in any direction, has its own momentum. It takes a lot of energy to stop and then to reverse. To begin with, he'd have to persuade David. Perhaps he wouldn't need much persuading. Could be he was having second thoughts as he drove down the road that crossed Wanstead Flats, the grassed area, dark and empty to the dim street lights on the other side. Jack knew it on a Sunday morning, full of the yells and energy of football players. He could make out no movement in its flat sleepiness. Though he did know a guy who went running in the early hours. Let's hope he was done and gone.

There was little other traffic, and that was disturbing. They were too obvious on the road, so late. So early.

They were grown ups, they had a choice. That's what the law said, unless you were mad. Though it could be argued this mission was a sort of madness. Though that wouldn't wash in a court of law. They could keep driving, keep up the bravado, the devil may care option. Do the knightly duty to the fair lady. And bury the body in the woods. Or, as law-abiding citizens, they could take the body back to the place of the crime, phone the police. And they'd be in the clear. More or less.

There'd be some awkward questions about all the moving of the body. It wouldn't look good. But what they were doing, if caught, would look a hundred times worse. They were in the hands of chance. So much could go wrong on this simple enterprise.

They turned into Wanstead High Street, heading towards Snaresbrook. The shops were shuttered, not a soul on the street. David knew the way. And didn't need Frank's Satnav. In fact, all the better, David said not to write in the journey.

It would be stuck in the history, and if it ever came to it, forensics could trace the route back to the house.

Forensics, for fuck's sake, thought Jack. Fibres and DNA all over the place. Over himself, the flat, the hallway. The body and the bag. So much to think about. Wiping off fingerprints in the car. It would be found, sooner or later.

'There's a cop behind,' exclaimed David. 'He's flashing me to stop.'

'Oh bugger,' said Jack. Mischance on their tail, with a loaded dice.

'Just keep calm,' said David as he pulled over. 'It can't be much.'

They'd stopped by the roadside. The police car pulled up behind. David let his window down as the police officer got out and walked to their car. He was in uniform with a flat cap. A young man, tall.

He bent down to speak. 'You know, you were speeding back there, sir.'

'Sorry, officer,' said David. 'Nothing else on the road, I hardly noticed.'

The officer looked around the car.

'What are you doing out this time of night?'

'I'm a cab driver,' said David. 'This is my fare.' He indicated Jack beside him.

The officer looked to Jack.

'Might I ask what you're doing up so late, sir?'

'I've been at my astronomy club,' said Jack, thinking quickly. 'Looking at the moon. You don't get many nights as clear as this,' he burbled, 'and with the moon in its third quarter it's a good time to take photos of craters near the terminator...'

'What's Arnie Schwarzenegger doing up there?'

For a second, Jack didn't know what the man was talking about. Then it clicked and he saw the policeman smiling.

'Good one,' he said with a half grin, the best he could manage. 'The terminator is the line between light and dark.

I'll show you.' He had his phone out and was fiddling with pictures he'd taken with Mia last night, trying to still the shake in his hands. 'There. That group of craters. See how the shadow makes 'em stand out.'

'Yeh,' said the policeman, nodding. 'That's pretty good for a phone...'

'Got better ones back at the club,' he said. 'With a proper astro camera.'

The policeman turned to David and bit his lip thoughtfully. 'Speeding though. I don't smell drink on you.'

'No, officer. This is my livelihood. Drinking is out of the question. And I was hardly over the speed limit.'

The officer thought for a few seconds. Jack wondered whether David was going to be breathalysed, just to check. Then there'd be all the hassle with driving licences... And the cop would find out this wasn't David's car. And they'd have to come up with more lies. All it needed was a request to open the boot. And then it was all up. He held his breath. And hoped.

'I should book you for speeding,' said the young policeman, scratching the side of his neck. 'You were doing 35 miles per hour in a built up area, maybe a bit more... But you were no danger, there's no traffic and you are sober. So rather than inflict myself with an hour's paperwork – drive on. And count yourself lucky. But I suggest you stick to the speed limit, sir.'

They thanked him profusely.

The policeman left. And they drove off, with David keeping a close eye on the speed. Maggie had driven ahead some way and stopped. She allowed them to come past and then followed in their wake.

Chapter 32

Anne took the sofa. She had Bessie scrubbing the carpet. And was impressed. The girl was down on all fours scrubbing away, specifically the bloody bits, she'd told her. Go over and over them. Scrub every last bit out.

And she was certainly working at it, a washing up bowl full of suds at her side.

Anne gathered up the bits of glass. She put them on the table in a heap as she picked them up, like a magpie collecting treasure. Her intention was to wrap them in newspaper before putting them in a bin bag. The glass had got everywhere, first by the bashing, and then exacerbated by Jack moving the sofa to drag the body out of the room.

She wondered how they were getting on. Had they got to the forest yet? Did police patrol it late at night, for just such events?

What a lot she'd thrown on everyone!

Just suppose she had called the police immediately. Then sat there until they'd come. She could hardly imagine that, but suppose. Then what?

She certainly knew some of it from her past experience. Her flat would become a crime scene for at least a few days. She could say goodbye to her current nursery children. They'd have to find other providers, and would they then come back to a premises where someone had been killed? If, that is, she were free for them to come back.

She would be taken to the station for questioning. They'd tell her she could have a lawyer present. And then it would begin. It wouldn't take them long to find who she was. Her past form. And might they then suspect that she had really murdered her husband six years ago? And here she was doing it again.

A serial killer.

Who'd fooled them once. They'd make sure she didn't this time.

Or could there be another tale? Frank certainly was a racist and a bully. She could get witnesses to that. Maybe he had a police record. Even for rape? Why should she be the first?

Yes, there could have been others. But instead, she was in a third tale. A buried body in the forest... Over which she had no control. They could do it well or badly. She was here, they were there. Dependent.

The corpse could stay buried forever, undiscovered, rotting to nothing. Or be found... And then what? That depended whether it was in a week or ten years. They'd emptied his pockets. So no easy trace, unless there was something they'd overlooked; there was often something. And the car that he had was just being dumped – how long before that was picked up and cops came here asking questions?

So many complexities. They were giving her a headache.

Bessie was singing tunelessly. The poor girl was happy. Anne had done someone some good. Though there'd be complications there as well, with the service charge for the flat coming in and bills for gas and electricity. How would all that get paid? The girl had no money. And even if Frank had, she couldn't get at it. Officially, he was still alive.

A tangle was growing. In the meantime, pick up glass, scrub the sofa. And look after Bessie. She had a duty there. Do something for the girl. Time someone did. Then if all this went wrong, at least she could say...

What a mess of an evening!

Dinner with a builder, such a good start. All the cooking and planning and dressing up... Then he'd arrived and it was all going so well. And if Jack hadn't had to run off to rescue his daughter, Frank would never have got in. Or if he had, would have been seen off. They'd have had a wonderful meal. Talked and talked, ended up in bed making love, and so on and so forth. Violins and sunsets. A honeymoon in the Caribbean.

And maybe somewhere, in an alternative universe, that was what was progressing. Instead of gathering glass, cleaning blood off the carpet and sofa, and burying a body in the woods, she and Jack were spooned together, sleeping the night away.

Chapter 33

They lifted the body out of the boot and laid it on the ground. Maggie was with them. They were in a car park on the edge of the forest. Really, just a muddied clearing, on a side road off the Epping New Road. It was raining slightly and the moon was covered in cloud, just showing as a glow in smudgy charcoal.

David said, 'I want to get rid of his car. If that policeman had asked for my driving licence...'

'Yeah,' agreed Jack. 'We'd have got ourselves knotted in lies.'

'There's another car park half a mile back. Let's leave the body in the forest temporarily. Dump his car, then come back here.'

'I don't like leaving the body,' said Maggie.

'There's no one about,' insisted David. 'It'll be safe enough. Why should anyone look in the forest?'

Maggie agreed reluctantly.

David and Jack carried the body, Maggie walked ahead with the torch shining downwards. They went in perhaps fifty metres, and found a thick holly tree. They dragged the corpse underneath the low foliage, and covered it in leaves. The party then walked back out to the car park.

David and Jack drove ahead in Frank's Aurora. Maggie followed in hers. The road was deserted. It was not a main road through the forest but a side road off the arterial. Fairmead Road, wherever that was. David seemed to know his way and kept his speed down. And Jack didn't comment. He felt somewhat safer, now unencumbered. Nothing to be found in their boot by any prying cop.

'Don't you wonder why we are doing this?' he said.

'I've been thinking about nothing else,' said David.

'Be a bastard, taking the body back now,' said Jack.

'I am most definitely not driving anywhere with a body in the boot,' exclaimed David. 'That copper had me shitting bricks. Though that was fast thinking, your moon stuff.'

'You as taxi driver was pretty sharp.'

'Black man, driving this late. What else could I be?'

They drew into the car park with Maggie following.

'We need to give the inside a good wiping,' said David. 'What have you got?'

'Nothing,' said Jack. 'We emptied everything out of his damned bloody car.'

'Maggie'll have something.'

She had a box of tissue in hers. They took a handful each and wiped the inside of Frank's car. The steering wheel, the seating, the door handles, the fascia, the windows. Maggie wiped down the boot, both inside and outside. And finally, the door handles were wiped clean.

They stepped away from the vehicle as if it were red hot.

Maggie collected the used tissues and was about to put them in a nearby litter bin.

'Not this one,' said Jack. 'Just in case.'

She nodded.

'I'm half asleep,' she yawned. 'Let's get this job done with.'

They piled into her car and drove back to the first car park. There, Maggie put the dirty tissues in a litter bin, going to the trouble of pushing them deep down into the detritus. And then cleaned her hands on a wipe. She offered them round.

'When we've done,' said Jack, refusing a wipe.

'Why the fuck aren't we wearing gloves?' said David.

'Because, darling,' said Maggie sweetly, 'we've never done this before.'

And Jack thought, sod it, he'd known he needed gloves, to hold the string round the bag. He'd thought of it earlier and forgotten in the bustle of leaving the house. Too bad now. They were here with what they had, not what they wanted.

They headed back into the forest to retrieve the corpse. It was easier without their burden. Maggie was ahead with the torch, David had the spades which Maggie had thoughtfully tied together.

They came to the holly tree. Jack and David ducked under its canopy.

'It's gone!' exclaimed Jack, scrabbling about.

'Can't have done,' cried David as he kicked old leaves.

'Shut up, the two of you,' hissed Maggie.

'Someone's taken the body,' said Jack. 'While we were at the other car park...'

'I don't believe it,' cried David. 'Ten minutes, fifteen at most, we were gone.'

They were groping about in the tent of the holly tree, down on their knees, swishing the leaves.

Maggie came under with the torch and shone it in their faces.

'You pair of idiots!' she exclaimed. 'Wrong tree.'

They came out.

She shone the torch a little way ahead. 'That one.'

They found the body there with little trouble, and pulled it out onto the path.

'Let's carry it sideways,' said Jack, 'then no one has to walk backwards.'

David took the head, Jack the legs, holding it under the strings. The path was wide enough for them to handle their package sideways. Maggie took the lead, the two spades over a shoulder and the torch in her free hand. She held the beam downwards. The order was not to chatter, only essential talk.

The way was shadowy, half-bare trees silhouetted against the night sky. The path was rutted with cycle tracks, boot prints and horseshoes. In places it was wet and muddy. Here they had to take care, go slow or go round, with Maggie directing them.

They had to stop for a minute or so, from time to time, to get the string stress out of their hands. Jack cursed himself for forgetting gloves. So obvious. What else had he forgotten?

After about quarter of an hour, Jack said, 'Let's get off the main drag and find somewhere to bury it.'

They took a narrow path where Jack had to walk backwards with Maggie just ahead leading him. They went along the path for a few minutes, brambles and twigs pressing in. At a clearer patch they stopped. And put down the body for a break.

'We have to go off track,' said Maggie.

David wiped his brow with his sleeve, breathing heavily. 'Weighty bugger. That string is cutting my hands in half,' he said. 'I must go to the gym again.'

Jack too was feeling the effort but was in better shape. This was manual work and he did plenty of that without the need of a gym. His hands were more calloused but the string still bit.

They left the path and headed into the thicket. The density made it slow work, ducking under branches, pushing through undergrowth. About a hundred metres away from the path, in an area free of trees, they stopped and put down their burden.

'Good a place as any,' said Jack.

Maggie cut the strings round the spades and gave them one each. Jack cleared away the fallen leaves on a patch of ground and tested the earth under it with a spade. With some hard pushing from his boot, it went into the fullness of the blade.

'Let's get digging,' he said.

They dug for a couple of hours. There were tree roots to impede them, the ground was claggy in places. And then came the difficulty of standing and digging in the hole with two spades as the hole got deeper. And so they had to take it in shifts. It was drizzling, not at all heavily, but enough that over time they were soaked through. David was plainly exhausted, Jack pushed on making his shifts longer, though he was tired enough. He knew the body needed to be at least a couple of feet down to evade discovery, and that meant a hole at least three feet in depth. Deeper still was better.

The inky sky was paling to a metallic blue when they decided they were deep enough. The body was dropped in. They had a brief discussion about whether to remove the bag from the corpse, but decided that would be too messy. They could make holes in it, allowing air and bugs in, so it would rot in time. With some pushing and pulling of the bag and contents, they were satisfied, as they ever might be, that it was down in the hole as low as they could get it. Holes were ripped in the plastic with Jack's knife. A waft of sweat and sour meat hit him as he tore.

Then the burial began. The two of them spading the earth back. Every so often, stopping to stomp in the earth, pushing soil into the crevices around the bagged corpse. And then back to the navvying effort of throwing earth on top.

There was birdsong. A blackbird, thought Jack, and others he didn't know. The moon had long since set and the sky was lightening. He should've brought his thermos; tea would've been a welcome break. This primitive, ageless work. Graves were dug by tractor diggers these days. No wonder. He felt sorry for Maggie sitting in a huddle, resting against a tree, her knees pulled to her round belly. Digging at least kept you warm.

At one point, Jack wondered whether anyone else was in the forest doing the same. Were they alone? An eerie thought for an eerie enterprise. Three upright citizens burying a body, and maybe East End gangsters somewhere nearby doing the same.

When the hole was filled to ground level, there was soil

left over. They scattered it in the woodland, taking spadefuls ten, fifteen metres away. And finally, they scraped leaf mould over the grave.

'Would anyone know?' said David, resting exhausted on his spade.

'Hardly,' said Jack. 'And not with a bit of weathering.'

Maggie had carved a T in a nearby tree.

'Why a T?' asked David.

'Why anything?' said Jack.

They were walking back slowly, Jack and David carrying a spade each. Maggie had the torch, but had switched it off, the beam had almost faded to nothing. And dawn was well on the way.

'I started doing an F,' said Maggie. 'Then I realised that would help identify him. Should he be found. So I changed it to a T.'

'And why should we need it?' said Jack.

'In case we ever have to come back,' said Maggie.

'Not till Hell freezes over,' exclaimed David, an arm pressing his aching back. 'The quicker I forget the stupidity of tonight the better.'

Chapter 34

They all got in Maggie's car for the drive back, Frank's having been dumped in the other car park. Maggie drove, and they were quickly onto the Epping New Road, driving south, heading back to East London. They passed the junction with Rangers Road, heading for Woodford Wells. Jack knew where he was now. Not that far from where he'd been the other night with Mia and the telescope. A more innocent enterprise.

'Suppose a cop stops us,' said David. 'Where do we say we have been?'

'A night walk in the forest,' said Jack in the back seat, striving to keep his eyes open.

'With Maggie six months pregnant?' exclaimed David.

'It's not an illness, officer,' explained Maggie, as if talking to a police officer. 'I'm perfectly fit and well. And exercise is good for pregnant women.'

'I wouldn't believe you,' said David.

'Got a better idea?'

'We could have been to see someone...' he began.

Jack interrupted him. 'Forget that. They'd ask names and addresses. A forest walk is nice and anonymous. Keep it simple. Let 'em think we're crazy.'

'We most definitely are,' said Maggie.

'But on a week day?' insisted David. 'With all three of us working. It's stupid.'

'They can't check on it,' said Jack. 'Better than you being a taxi driver.'

'Suppose the same cop stops us?' exclaimed David.

Jack was picking up David's fear. The same cop and they'd be screwed by their earlier lies.

'Just drive below the limit,' he said. 'It's not likely he'll be about.'

'None of this is likely,' said David wearily. 'But here we are. Having buried a corpse in Epping Forest, trying to come up with an alibi.'

Conversation stopped. All three caged in their dreads. The unlikely could always happen. Made the more likely with so little traffic. And what David said was so true. Unless you were on holiday, you wouldn't go for a night walk in Epping Forest on a week night. Tell that one and they are bound to be suspicious. Bound to investigate further.

There were so many of them involved. The whole thing was nutty. One could keep a secret, perhaps. But six of them? At least only three of them knew where the body was. Make that two, he'd had no idea where he'd been in the forest.

They were back in Wanstead, running past the shuttered shops. The ink was draining from the sky, black shapes getting colour. Jack watched out for police cars. It was near here they'd been stopped on the way out. There were a few early workers walking on the pavement. And a few cars. They weren't quite so obvious.

Turning out of the high road, they took the quiet street above the M11 link road for quarter of a mile, and then turned into Blake Hall Road. On another night, he might've enjoyed the ride, a trip from night into day. But he was too eager to be off the road, to not risk dodgy explanation. Lies.

They were crossing Wanstead Flats, there was a little more traffic. The trees in the middle were visible and the brick, barrack-style changing room. The world was waking up. A bus with people on came by, real people. And into Forest Gate where pedestrians were heading for the station. They were safe. Another car amongst cars.

The Co-op was open, and Greggs bakery and the paper shop.

By the time they were again at the house, it was day. And the street lights had turned off.

Maggie and David rushed upstairs to prepare for work. Jack knocked on Anne's door. She opened up, surprisingly fresh, showered, in jeans and a blue T-shirt. She invited him in.

'How did it go?'

He shrugged. 'The bastard's buried in Epping Forest. His car is dumped. Let's hope that's that.'

He went into the sitting room. It was tidy and organised. All the remnants from the killing removed or washed away. Bessie was asleep in the armchair, a blanket over her, her head in a corner against a cushion.

'She was working like a Trojan,' said Anne quietly. 'I had to stop her.'

Jack was looking at the sofa where the body had lain. There were faint traces of blood, like the outline of an unknown country. He ran his finger round it.

'I scrubbed for hours on that,' exclaimed Anne. 'Do you think that's good enough?'

'Good enough for me,' he said. 'I'd not spot it normally. But the law... if they were looking... Maybe they could get his DNA out of that.' He shrugged. 'I don't know.'

'There's some on the rug too,' she said.

She showed him a barely visible trace on the rug, just below the sofa. He kneeled down for a closer look. He could barely think, he was so knackered. And yet there was a day ahead. It had all been so continuous.

'We should get rid of the rug and sofa,' he said.

She looked at her watch. 'I've got the first kids coming in half an hour.'

'My skip is still out there, due to be picked up tomorrow morning. Let me put the rug on it,' he said.

'I dumped my torn dress in it, that blood stained thing I was wearing,' she said.

'You'd better put anything else you were wearing in too. They can pick up the finest of traces.' And added with a wry, 'So my TV watching of CSI tells me.'

'I could make you some breakfast,' she said.

'That'd be great.'

She kissed him on the cheek. 'Thank you, Jack.'

He flapped a hand in dismissal. 'Don't thank me. If you're caught then so am I.'

'Sorry.'

What response was there to that? He had buried a body in the forest and dumped a car. For a woman he hardly knew. Liked, found attractive. What loneliness can do.

'Make the breakfast,' he said. 'I'll take the carpet out.'

She left him.

He moved the furniture to free the carpet, trying to do so as quietly as possible so as not to wake Bessie, but unfortunately her armchair was on a corner of the rug. He tipped her chair back, pulled the rug out – and her bleary eyes opened.

'Good morning, Bessie.'

'What am I doing here?' she said feebly. 'Oh yes, I was helping Anne...'

He didn't want to mention the burying of the body and so forth, not sure how she'd react.

She said, 'Has he gone?'

'Gone forever.'

'I did it,' she said.

Not that again, he thought. But he was not going to argue.

'I've got to take the carpet out,' he said.

'I scrubbed it and scrubbed it. Just couldn't get that last bit out,' she declared.

'The room's very clean,' he said.

'We washed the whole flat,' she said. 'Everything. And I want to do my place. It is mine now. And scrub him out of it. Do all the sheets, specially the sheets, the duvet, throw his porny computer away...'

'Good for you, Bessie.'

He was rolling up the rug. She got up and stretched.

Then folded the blanket as Anne opened the hatch from the kitchen.

'Morning, Bessie. Just making breakfast. Scrambled egg on toast?'

'Only a bit,' said Bessie.

Jack took the rug out to the skip. The street was awake with traffic and pedestrians, though this was not the busiest of roads. He was like a zombie, head scooped out in living death, merely able to do automatic things.

The skip was almost full with the brickwork from the wall. Some he'd left in the garden, to be used as rubble for fixing the fence posts in. It was fortunate he'd allowed another day for skip removal as this firm came early. He moved some of the bricks to make room for the carpet and saw the carrier bag with Anne's dress in it. He pushed it further in.

Maggie ran out of the house, changed and showered. She stopped by the skip where Jack was.

'Don't know how I'm going to cope with today,' she exclaimed. 'David is utterly exhausted, but he's going in anyway. Says he'll stare at a screen and look busy. And drink gallons of coffee on the house. Must go.'

She gave a wave and swept away, surprisingly energetic considering. But then she was goal centred, had a position to keep up.

He put the rug in the skip. Tomorrow it would all go and be dumped in landfill, forever and ever. Amen. Buried under more and more rubbish, all the squalor of city living. He rolled his shoulders and twisted his neck. All that digging after a day's work, no sleep, he was tired before the day began. How much would he get done in this state?

He noted then that his fencing had come with the concrete pillars and bags of cement, all by the garden door. Too bloody efficient, that outfit. More humping and lifting. Breakfast first, before he dealt with that lot. But best not leave them out. Too many light fingers round here.

Chapter 35

Jack felt more alive after he'd eaten. Two cups of coffee had given him a charge of energy. Anne's children had arrived and she was in childminder mode, fully occupied. Jack had decided to take the sofa away but had to get the fencing gear in the garden first. It didn't pay to be too trusting. You could go out somewhere, come back an hour later and find it all gone.

He barrowed the fencing, posts and cement into the garden. The cement he put in the shed in case it should rain again. The rest would survive the elements. They had a ten year guarantee. Though who would remember in nine years? He'd be long gone, and so might the fence company.

Bessie helped him carry out the sofa. She delighted in being helpful, though she wasn't that strong, and he had to go at her speed. Life was going to change for her with her old man dead. Or missing. It was complicated, her situation, too complicated to dwell on. For today anyway.

It was impossible to get the sofa up on the roof rack, which made him increasingly crotchety with each failed attempt. He was determined to be rid of the sofa and its damning stains. Bessie just couldn't lift her end high enough, though she tried hard. And he really had to bite his tongue to stop himself yelling at her. The last thing she needed.

They'd just have to take it back in to Anne's.

Fortunately, David came out of the house just then. And Jack collared him at once. David was wearing a smart grey suit, and at first bridled at the work offered, but, seeing the fix they were in, relented. The three of them got it on the roof. And David dashed off.

Jack tied the sofa onto his roof rack with a long length of rope.

'Want to come with?' he said to Bessie.

'Can I?' she said, as if amazed to be asked.

'Of course.'

'I never go anywhere,' she said. 'Where are we going?'

'China,' he said. 'Or maybe Brazil. What about Tierra Del Fuego?'

'Where's that?'

'Near Ilford.'

He told Anne they'd be a while and set off. The plan was to take the sofa to a charity shop a few miles off. Out of this area, so there'd be no connection.

Bessie was pleased to be in the van. Jack realised this was an outing for her. She never went anywhere beyond the local shops. He turned the music on for her, the CD he had already in. He couldn't remember what it was, and as soon as he heard the first few bars he had it. Blur.

'I like this one,' she said.

'The track's called *For Tomorrow*, from the Blur album *Modern Life Is Rubbish*.' The title amused him, considering all that had happened in the last 12 hours. And then he was la-la-la-ing in the chorus, quite light-headed. He'd had this one ages. Amazing it still worked. Amazing he still played it. 'The first album I bought,' he said. 'Had to buy it. Well, I tried to nick it from Woolworths, but ended up with an empty album case. I was only a kid.'

'I've heard of Blur,' she said.

The traffic was busy, still rush hour, as they headed up the Romford Road towards Ilford. The nose to tail cars irritated him but it was sightseeing for Bessie. And she was enjoying the music. Well, why not? But he was supposed to be earning a living.

Soon as he'd dumped this sofa.

After being stuck in a jam for five minutes, hardly moving, he suggested they get a coffee at Manor Park.

Not the brightest of thoughts, as Jack had trouble parking. But he'd made the offer and didn't want to disappoint. He found a space on a side road as a woman was leaving it. They walked to a nearby workman's café.

Bessie had a hot chocolate, he a cup of tea. He thought, how is she going to manage with no money? Her father, monster that he was, at least paid for food and bills. And, as far as the world was concerned, still was paying. Presumably he had a bank account, owned the flat and was responsible for its bills.

But six people knew him to be dead.

At some time or other, he would become a missing person. Say a week or so. They would have to report him. And hopefully, he'd stay a missing person. In which case who would his flat belong to? And when could a missing person be legally considered dead?

He said none of this, barely understanding the complications himself. Today's stuff to be dealt with first. He asked her about her schooling and the music she liked. School she'd hated, as for music, all the poppy stuff. She could listen when her father was out of the house.

They set off again. Headed further up the Romford Road to Ilford. The traffic had lightened, at least it was moving. They passed under the concrete span North Circular to another track from *Modern Life Is Rubbish*. Sometimes it is, and sometimes it isn't. Currently he wasn't sure, as they came up the hill to Ilford.

Jack knew there were charity shops that took furniture on Cranbrook Road. He told Bessie to keep a lookout as he turned into it. She was eagerly watching both sides and a little way up spotted a British Heart Foundation shop with furniture in the window. They parked and Jack ran inside. It was a huge place with lots of sofas, sideboards, wardrobes, beds and so forth. He asked a young man if they wanted a sofa. The young man called the manageress. She came outside and looked at it. Jack hoped they wouldn't reject it.

That would be a hassle. But apart from the slight, barely visible staining, it was almost as new. The manageress looked at it quizzically. Jack didn't say anything, wondering what her standards were.

'We'll take it,' she said.

'All yours,' said Jack. 'Can we have some help getting it down?'

She went inside and came out again with a couple of young men. Jack untied the sofa, helped them get it to ground level, and left them to carry it away. He thought about buying another one for Anne here. Then rejected it. Why would someone bring in an almost new sofa and then buy another one, probably inferior? That would be too memorable.

So they left without any further load.

And drove a little further, and found another charity furniture shop, where they bought a sofa for Anne.

Chapter 36

Anne didn't think much of the sofa, but what could she say but 'very nice, Jack'. She felt it such an awful green, an attempt to be foresty but too dense and artificial. And it fitted with nothing in her room. Why on earth did the idiot buy her a sofa anyway? Plainly, he had no colour sense. Well, she'd have to keep it a while now. Obligated. Yes, it was something to sit on. She could get some covers for it.

Looking on the bright side on a tired morning, the stained one had gone. This would do for the time being. It would have to. Though every time she looked at it she thought of the pretty one that had gone. She knew she shouldn't blame Jack. He was just trying. She was in a filthy, ratty mood. Lack of sleep, obviously.

'Fine, fine,' she enthused. 'It will fill the hole.'

Bessie was keeping an eye on the children while they had a coffee in the sitting room. Trying out the sofa.

She doesn't like it, thought Jack. Bollocks to her then. After all he'd done this morning. Women! Alison had never let him buy any furniture either. He'd once come back with some new curtains, which ended up a week later, not even unpacked, going to Oxfam. Dumb of him. Anne hadn't asked for it. He'd simply thought, while I'm out, surprise her.

Next time, don't bother.

She looked fresh and attractive, objectively attractive that was to say, for in his spaced out zone he simply knew it from hearsay. An alien being told him that's what attractive women on Earth looked like. In this room, he couldn't see beyond her bloody face and torn dress. And was too whacked out to say anything beyond platitudes. Anything else would come out wrong. There'd be a fight.

He caught himself. What had she just said? He grunted as if he knew. Knew fuck all about anything. This vomit stew he was swimming in. It was stupid staying here, pretending to be alive.

He rose and said, 'I'm going home. I've got to get some sleep.'

She pecked him on the cheek, he twitched and hoped she hadn't noticed.

'Do you want to come back this evening?' she said as she saw him to the door. Something to say, automatically, expected of her. She was relieved when he cried off, pleading exhaustion. She thought she might like him again tomorrow. The sofa might look better. The day, the future, her life, might all improve. Tomorrow.

When he'd gone, she sat on the sofa for a few minutes to finish her coffee. It was such a strain to talk, to pretend, to act out a way you are expected to feel but don't. She would crack so easily if she were a spy. A day or two without sleep and she'd be spilling the names of comrades and lovers. How awful she was when it came down to it. Her life was one big lie.

The next she knew, she was waking up. Her thigh was wet and the sofa by her. A coffee cup was smashed on the floor. She'd evidently fallen asleep. Simply switched off. How long? She had no idea.

The children!

She rushed into the nursery. It was an isle of tranquillity. No one dead. The baby was in the playpen drinking juice from a bottle. Bessie was in the story area, the two twins leaning against her as she read them *Where The Wild Things Are*.

She said, 'Sorry, Bessie. I fell asleep.'

Bessie looked up from her book and smiled. 'I've read this three times to them.'

'They do like it,' said Anne weakly.

Her thigh was sticky. She remembered the broken china in the living room. The two twins were protesting at the grown ups talking. Bessie continued from where she'd left off.

Anne said, 'I spilt some coffee. I've got to clean up. Give me five minutes.'

Bessie nodded without breaking her reading.

Chapter 37

Nancy had got up late. Not that it mattered, she wasn't going anywhere. Bingo was tomorrow, and just the afternoon. She'd been woken by Tickles mewling. She normally fed him first thing and here he was, hungry. She was so pleased he was healthy and hungry after the horror of last night. And she must give that builder some money for getting that tack out of his throat. It would've killed him.

She watched her cat eat. And thought, there's nothing wrong with you, boy. All that kerfuffle last night. Going out into the garden to finish the spell which she'd never really believed in, but here he was, Bessie's father, dead. Did that mean Bessie and she had killed him? Or was it just coincidence?

It didn't matter; either way a mean man had gone out of her life. No more kicks on the stairs for Tickles, and insults and humiliations for her. She'd slept so well, Tickles warm on her bed.

Through her front window she'd seen Bessie and the builder struggling with the sofa. All that trouble getting it on the van, almost like one of those silly films. Picking it up, putting it down. Lucky they got some help from David. She wondered where they were taking it. And then later on they came back with another one. Busy morning.

She half listened to the radio for a bit while she read one of her magazines. She needed to get Bessie to buy her the latest. Watched a little television, *Bargain Hunt*, that was always good fun. And waited for Bessie to come up. The cat litter was smelling. It did mean Tickles was healthy though. Both ends working, as they say.

Bessie didn't come up till mid afternoon. And she'd washed her hair and had it cut.

She said, 'I did it at Anne's, in her bathroom. She gave me a shampoo. She showed me how to use a hair dryer. And then she cut it for me. In between looking after the children. Oh, that Dominic, he wanted to do it. 'Scissors, scissors, gimme scissors...' he kept saying. But then she got them painting, and was able to finish me off.' She turned about. 'Do you like it?'

'It's much better, dear. The brown shows up nicely, and she's cut it well.'

'Dad used to do it,' said Bessie. 'Always him. We never had shampoo after Mum went, just soap. I do like the hairdryer, it's so warm on the head and face. Do you think men will stare at me, Nancy?'

'With a new dress, and maybe a visit to the dentist...'

'Anne phoned the dentist for me. Got me an appointment for next week. I'm frightened. Last time I went Mum took me,' she said. 'I was just a kid then. I remember all that drilling and poking about in my mouth...' She stopped. 'Now I've got to be quick with you, because Anne wants me to help out.'

'Oh, it's Anne this, Anne that. Has she got you now?'

'I'll come back this evening, promise. We can watch TV together. Now Dad won't be back.'

This satisfied Nancy. An evening visitor would be a very nice thing.

Bessie emptied the cat litter and put in the new. And then went out to buy a magazine for Nancy who told her to buy something nice to snack on for their evening viewing.

Chapter 38

It happened on the way home. Traffic was sluggish, stop start, on Upton Lane, and he nodded off for a couple of seconds. Just long enough to cross a red light and hit a car going across. Fortunately he wasn't going fast, but Jack dented the door of the car he hit, broke one of his car headlights and buckled a wing.

Jack apologised to the woman, without admitting he'd fallen asleep at the wheel. That would be criminal and he wasn't setting himself up for that. She was middle-aged, a white collar professional judging by her suit, and very angry.

'Right through a red light,' she harangued. 'Were you on the phone?'

At least he could give a negative to that accusation.

'Are you registered blind? Red, clear red, it was!'

He had no arguments, and admitted his guilt. There was no way out of it, hitting her on the side – plus she had a couple of witnesses. He gave his insurance details, his name and address, showed her his licence. There was no point being difficult. He was exhausted, shouldn't be on the road, and was lucky it wasn't a major accident.

Just a damned nuisance.

Up would go his insurance. He'd have to pay the first £200 of the damages. Bollocks. And his own repair would mean he'd be without his van for however long it took. It was drivable still, but not at night.

The shock had woken him completely. Just a few blinks of unseeing – and smash. What if he had been going faster, what if Mia were with him?

He should have walked home. It was only fifteen minutes

away from where he was working. Common sense said leave the van and foot it. You get used to driving everywhere. Get in the van when you have to go up the road to get a sandwich. Always in a rush. Habit. Shagged out, he was a menace on the road.

All that money down the drain.

At least no one was hurt. And no witnesses to his nodding off. So with relief, he considered, it was just money. Just! But he'd not argue about paying it. He knew drivers who would self righteously lie their way out of any accident, no matter how culpable. But this was clean and clear. It was his fault; he should've walked, tired as he was. Plain and clear, he should not have been driving.

It was only money. No blood this time round. Be grateful.

Two hundred quid – and so preventable.

He got home without further incident. And reported the accident at once to his insurance. Otherwise, the state he was in, he knew he'd forget. And simply slumped, fully clothed, on the bed.

And couldn't sleep, irony of ironies. He could at the wheel, but not on the mattress. His mind was too active, flying everywhere, going over and over the events of the night. Bagging the body, the meeting in the nursery – almost comical in its bravado. Carrying the body to the car, the close shave with the cop, humping the corpse through the midnight forest and digging the grave until near dawn.

Like a film plot he'd been watching at the cinema, and then been pushed into the screen and forced to play it out.

The dinner with Anne, another century, another continent. But Anne's bloody face and ripped dress when she opened the door to him, that image repeated, like a loop in spacetime, the beautiful woman at the dinner table, over and over, to the butcher at the door.

'I've killed him, Jack.'

He didn't give a damn for Frank, not as a person, a living,

breathing human being, but for his part in the killing. The blood on his hands, the weight of the corpse, the burial in the forest. Time knew, time saw. Time had it in splatters.

After an hour of lying there, eyes closed in his cinema of guilt, Jack rose and showered. He went back to bed naked, and under the duvet pulled himself to the foetal position. He so wanted to sleep, but was too tired, his mind too speedy, too full.

A drink would work, fill himself with oblivion, drug himself away. Drink and drink, out and away. Until there was nothingness. No tumbling images of her living room and the dark forest. Nothing. Every sensation drowned.

And he remembered, like a straw pulled from a stack, what he'd been told in one of his counselling sessions; don't lie in a helpless position when you feel bad. You will only feel worse. And then you'll get drunk.

And then you'll be on the skids again.

He threw off the duvet, rose and got dressed. He did not want to go out, too many pubs and booze shops. Tried some television but couldn't take its trivia. Had a go at an astronomy magazine, but could do little beyond looking at the pictures. Tried music, loud with headphones; there was too much inside to pay attention to the outside.

He phoned Anne.

'Can I come over? I can't do anything here.'

'Please do,' she said. 'I'm in need of company.'

He walked over. The light was too bright, there was too much space. The world had too much in it. He must escape.

PART THREE:
THE BEST LAID PLANS

Chapter 39

Bert was opposite the house in his car and somewhat frustrated. He had two prime steaks on the seat beside him, and had phoned Frank repeatedly that day – and got no reply. The berk must've lost his phone or his battery was down.

It was annoying. He didn't want to be here on a wild goose chase. All he'd wanted to do was remind Frank about their dinner get-together, and now he was here, outside his house, and couldn't see his car. Still out and about on his taxi run.

He'd wait a while longer. Bound to be back soon. Better be. He'd said half five and it was already a quarter to. Bert hated waiting. If you say a time – be there. That was his mantra. Life's too short for hanging around.

He let his window down. The motor could do with a clean out. He had a tendency to throw things on the back seat or the floor. Take-outs, coffee, any old papers. Smelling a bit, except he'd got used to it. There was a blonde woman he had his eye on at England First. A real blonde, nothing bottled, a native northern European, total Aryan. Yes. He would get Frank's daughter on the clean up of the car, and then a hoover. Give her a couple of quid. While the men talked business.

There was a builder's skip outside the house and a woman looking in it. Quite a nice looking bit of work, hefty undercarriage. Oh, pregnant. Don't touch. You don't know who's been in there first. What was she looking at? Something worth having? No, she seemed to be pushing something further in.

He watched her leave the skip, change her mind and

come back to it, then with a piece of wood push whatever it was down further. Must be pretty smelly, he thought. Maybe a dead cat. Then she left the skip and went through the gate of the house, along the path and up the steps. And let herself in.

Then it clicked. Must be that woman who lives over Frank, pregnant with a half-caste baby. The one Frank had plans about. Her husband, or partner or whatever, had given him that shiner. As well to know what she looked like.

He glanced at his watch. He'd give him twenty minutes. You know, if you make a date with a mate, then it's up to you to be there, he'd lay it on the line. He was bringing the steaks for heaven's sake. Prime sirloin. And Bert was getting hungry.

A black man in a suit had gone up the steps and was at the door of the house. Look at him. Just out of the trees and dares to have a leather briefcase. No doubt full of bananas. That would be her husband, betcha. Couldn't she do better than that?

What is it with these white women?

The man was going through his pockets. Keys obviously. Every pocket: back, front, inside. Now his briefcase. Papers, how disappointing. Pockets again. No luck. He was ringing the bell. And someone was letting him in.

Not exactly high excitement.

A few more minutes and he'd had enough. All the fun of the skip and front door wasn't enough. He needed to find out what Frank was up to. Bert got out, locked his car and crossed the road. Had a glance in the skip where the woman had been poking. Something way down in a carrier bag. Dead baby perhaps?

Wishful thinking.

At the door, he pressed the entry-phone. Waited. Nothing. This was a right palaver. What's Frank up to? He pressed again, hard and long. And again, keeping his finger on it this time. Long and hard.

Bessie answered, 'Who is it?'

'It's Bert, your dad's mate. Why aren't you fucking answering the bell?'

'I was in the toilet.'

'Yeh, alright,' not sure whether to believe her. 'Is your dad there?'

'No, he's out.'

'Well I've got some steaks for us. You'd better let me in.' There was no response. Angrily he said, 'Did you hear me, gel? You'd better let me in.'

'He's not in,' she said.

'I know, you told me that already. Let me fucking in. He's expecting me. I'll wait up there. Don't piss me about. Let me in or I'll give you one you'll remember.'

The entry-phone buzzed. Bert pushed the door open, and walked in.

Chapter 40

'So, where is he?'

Bessie shrivelled in her shoes. 'Don't know, Bert.'

Bert was striding about the flat as if he owned it, pushing back his red hair, looking out the window every time he came to it.

'So when did you last see him?'

She was seated on one of the table chairs. He stopped above her. She was afraid he would hit her. And he would do a lot more if he knew.

'He didn't come home last night,' she said.

Bert stared hard at her. She was sure he was going to hit her now. It was somehow the wrong answer.

'So is he staying with someone?' he enquired.

'Don't know,' she said helplessly.

He bent down and almost spat in her face. 'You're a fucking lot of help.'

'Sorry,' she said feebly.

'Don't be fucking sorry.' He bit his thumb. 'Give me the number of his taxi firm.'

She was instantly up and got Bert a card which lay by the phone. He read it thoughtfully then took the house phone and dialled.

'Angelo Cabs,' said a female voice.

'I'm a bit worried about Frank Brand, one of your drivers, me and his daughter. We can't contact him and wondered whether he's out driving.'

'Frank hasn't been in today, sir. He should've been. But we've heard nothing from him.'

'Do you know since when?'

'One moment, sir.' He could just hear her asking others.

'Not since yesterday, early evening, sir.'

'Thanks for your help,' said Bert and put down the phone. He turned to Bessie, a fat lot of good she was, but then there was no one else. 'He's bloody well disappeared. Phone dead. Not at work. Something don't smell right.'

Chapter 41

Maggie was in an armchair, staring at the ceiling, eyes closed, a coffee on the arm.

'The kids were awful today,' she said wearily. 'And I was worse. Snapping and shouting. I never do that. I could see they were frightened stiff of me. All this term I've been building up a relationship with my class, trust and fairness... And today, I'm this out of control tyrant.' She took some coffee and grimaced. 'God, I've drunk so much of this bloody stuff. I must be pickled in it. So what the hell...' She greedily drank it all. 'The poor kid in here,' she rubbed her tummy, 'is going to spend a lifetime awake. Sorry, so sorry little 'un. I am utterly and totally spent.'

David was on the sofa flat out, his jacket and tie off, shirt sleeves rolled up. His stockinged feet were on one arm, his head against a cushion on the other, two hands pressed against his brow.

'I was OK until mid afternoon,' he said. 'And then it hit me like a hammer blow. I couldn't do a thing. I was so spaced out. I just left the shop. Had to. And went over to the park. And sat in the bandstand. Sat there as if I was part of the woodwork. I eventually came back – and I was supposed to have been at a meeting. I got Muriel to phone to say I had toothache. Imagine if I'd been interviewed for the area manager post this afternoon. The day's been endless...' He waved a helpless hand. 'And to top it all, I've lost my keys.'

'Where?' she said.

'If I knew where, I'd have found them,' he snapped.

'Not necessarily,' she countered.

'I had them when I came in last night from work,' he said stroppily. 'And then...' he slapped his forehead. '...didn't have them when we came back from the forest.' He sat up in alarm.

She jerked forward and stared at him.

'You saying you lost them in the forest?'

He was scratching his scalp agitatedly. 'When we were digging, I took my jacket off, hung it on a branch. Remember? Must be then. I bet you.'

'Are you sure? Might be in my car. Or here in the flat.'

'It must be there,' he said. 'When I was digging. Yes. I picked up my coat. I remember it hanging over the branch.' He nodded vigorously. 'That's where they are. Fell out of my pocket.'

'The keys with the Nigerian key fob?' she said.

'Yes,' he said, irritated. 'I don't have any others.'

'And you're certain?' she said, itemising, deliberate. 'There. Where we buried the body. You lost your keys.'

'I keep them in the outside pocket of my jacket.' He closed his eyes. 'I can see it now. I put the jacket over the branch... They're there. I know it.'

The two were silent. Seeing the forest. The keys. Someone in uniform picking them up.

'I can't believe it,' she exclaimed. 'Right where he is buried, my husband drops his keys. And just to make sure there's no doubt whose they are, he leaves the set with a Nigerian flag key fob. How clever!'

'I should've hung the jacket up properly...'

'There wasn't a coat hook, darling.'

'Oh fuck off!'

He was sunk down, his head in his hands.

'Wherever I go, whatever I do,' she said, 'that doesn't affect the keys.' She was pointing at the ground in the forest, her finger daggering. 'There, they will lie, week after week, year after year...'

'They'll get covered in leaves in no time,' he said. 'Sink into the ground.'

'So we are to rely on autumn leaves and earthworms?'

She stood up and pushed him back onto the sofa seat with both arms. 'Is that the best you can offer?'

'I'm knackered, darling. I can't handle this now. It's a big forest, it's a little key ring...'

She got down to his level, on her knees, and held his head between her hands.

'And I am shagged too, dearest. But I don't want to be jailed. Buried bodies show up. One day, maybe next week, next year or the year after... that body could be found. There will be a crime scene, with lots of crawling coppers and police tape. And they'll find your keys and put them in a little plastic bag. They'll identify the body, all those clever boffins in the lab. And they'll check who was living in his house at the time. And think to themselves who is most likely to have a key ring with a Nigerian flag fob? Oh yes, that Nigerian man.'

They were face to face, she staring into his dark eyes, their noses almost touching.

'And in case they have an iota of doubt they'll check the keys for DNA and fingerprints...' she continued, 'I don't know how long that stuff lasts. But I do know a Nigerian fob will last a fucking century.'

He pushed her away. 'Bollocks, bollocks, bollocks.'

She rose, swung round, grasped a magazine and hit him on the head with it.

'Think!' she said, 'if you're not too knackered. What will happen if we should be arrested? What might be the tariff? Two years in jail for perverting the course of justice or whatever they call it, four years? I shall of course never be able to teach again once I come out of Holloway. The only management position you'll get is chief of slopping out at Dartmoor...'

'They don't slop out anymore.'

She hit him on the head again. He grasped her wrist and twisted the magazine out of it with his other hand.

'Leave me alone, you bloody bitch!'

She smacked him round the face with her free hand.

'Look what you've done!' she was screaming, hopping around the room, pulling herself free of him. 'Prime suspects in a fucking murder case! Who says they won't hang it on you? You socked him in the eye. Might have murdered him here, in this flat, if we hadn't pulled you off him!'

'Don't be so damn clever after the fact, madam!' He was rubbing his face where she'd slapped him. 'You didn't say anything last night. You were all for helping Anne. I never heard you say,' he made a plaintive imitation of her, 'David, let's not. Instead it was, I'll drive. Just like a girl guide. Here's tissues, everyone, for wiping off your fingerprints... Thought of every fucking thing, didn't you?'

'Except when I married you,' she said.

'Oh oh, here we go. You're sounding just like your bloody mother. Her sweet princess from the shires marrying a black man... Call the West African Slave Company and take him away in chains.'

She was biting her knuckles. He was pressing his fingers into his palms, staring at the carpet. She sank onto a chair by the table. She was so angry, she was so miserable, she was so tired. A tear was coursing down her cheek. What on earth was happening? She was losing control, she never lost control, and David, her poor David, she had actually hit him...

'I am so sorry,' she said quietly.

'I'm sorry too.'

She sat down by him and took his hand. She squeezed gently, he squeezed back.

'Shouting never works, darling,' she said. 'I knew that at school today, I know that now. It's so stupid. Shout and you have lost it. And if I wasn't so tired...'

'I have to find those keys, Maggie,' he said, taking a deep breath.

'*We* have to,' she said.

'I'll take tomorrow off. Think of something to tell them. I don't know, food poisoning or whatever. And go to the forest and find those keys.'

'I'm coming with you.'

'You don't have to.'

'I don't want to spend two years in the nick because of those keys. I've also got food poisoning tomorrow. I can feel it coming on.'

Chapter 42

The onions were frying and his stomach was turning at the tang wafting from the kitchen. Bessie was cooking one of the steaks. He wasn't expecting Frank to come in with the beer. Something had happened. Surely Frank would have contacted him if he could?

This was supposed to be a planning meeting. Not a meal on his own. He mused over what he knew. Frank hadn't come home last night, and didn't go to work today. So, could be in a love nest, banging away. Such things were possible and if so, good luck to him, but then he should've phoned his mate. Mind you, such things make you forgetful.

Could be in hospital. Car accident or whatever. And lost his phone.

Bert thought of fucking his daughter. With her hair done, she wasn't so bad. But he didn't know how Frank would take that. With his own sister, he made sure guys had respect. No liberties. So best keep his flies done up round Bessie. For now at least.

The steak was sizzling, the aroma slopped in his mouth. Well, he'd make the most of a good meal. Take pleasure when it's offered.

There were footsteps above. He looked to the ceiling. And raised voices. Must be the couple Frank was going on about, the ones he'd seen earlier, him black with a briefcase, her white and pregnant.

'That mixed couple upstairs,' he shouted, 'do they row often?'

'Never,' she called.

He thought, this isn't never. And it sounded pretty heavy. He poked his head in the kitchen.

'I'm just going to have a listen upstairs,' he said.

She wasn't due any explanation, being only Bessie. But his steak was cooking and he wanted her to know he wasn't going far.

Bert went out of the flat, keeping the door ajar. He could hear the shouting above as he crept up the stairs. Mostly her voice. She was loud, occasionally him. Once on their landing, he took the few steps to their door and put his ear against it.

It was hard to make sense of their row, coming in halfway, and some of the words lost. He wanted to bang on the door and yell – speak up. Something about keys and forest. Did he hear the word Frank? He was almost sure he did. He lost the next bit. Then coppers and Holloway. And he suddenly caught a line that stood out: 'Prime suspect in a fucking murder case!' They weren't yelling about a TV programme, bet your bottom dollar.

It went quiet in the flat. He could make out the odd murmuring but nothing much. Time for him to go, in case they came out and caught him at the door.

Bert crept down the stairs. He went into Frank's flat and shut the door, the smells from the kitchen making him aware how hungry he was.

He sat at the table, ready. She brought out his knife and fork, the mustard and ketchup. She was quite fanciable in her apron, her hair cut neat. Better if she didn't open her mouth with those yellow teeth. She came back with the main dish of steak, onions, mushrooms, fried potatoes and peas. He told her to go to her room while he ate.

She left him.

Murder and steak. Could it be right, what he was thinking? The sense he made of the fragments he'd heard was that the mixed couple had killed Frank and buried him in the forest. But might there be another tale he was missing? Could he have it totally wrong? Any minute Frank could walk in the door and tell him about the corker he'd been hammering.

But Frank hadn't been home last night, no phone contact, hadn't been to work, and a couple who never argued were going at it hammer and tongs. And yelling things, the scraps he'd got, that could mean dirty deeds in the forest.

Say what you like, she could make a fine steak. Eat it slow, enjoy. Pity there was no beer. Though he could send her out for a couple, even have the other steak if he wanted to pig it. And if he was half right about Frank, then his daughter would make a fruity afters.

Chapter 43

Anne and Jack were seated on the floor of the nursery, coffees beside them. They'd gone in the sitting room for a few minutes when he first arrived, but Jack felt uncomfortable in that place, and they came out here. The nursery had more openness with its large garden windows. The sun was setting in fiery clouds between the trees at the rear.

Anne had had another shower and had changed again, a yellow T-shirt and red jeans. The red made him uneasy, its brightness sexual and bloody. She was barefooted, her toenails painted pink. He suspected that was for him, to emphasise her small feet. Perhaps the shower and the clean clothes too. Perhaps not, rather she was washing away memory and smears. Her face was bright and pink, but couldn't disguise the weariness around her eyes.

The washing machine was purring away in the utility room. Jack suspected the hottest of washes for any remnant clothing from last night, but had no wish to ask. Though he should check just in case, as his fate was now bound up with hers.

She said, 'I fell asleep this afternoon, out here. God knows what could have happened with the kids if Bessie hadn't been around. She just took over, playing with them, reading them a story, giving them juice. If I'd been on my own...' She shuddered. 'Kids this age are so vulnerable. Can be such savages... A fall, a bashing with a toy.' She stretched and smiled ruefully. 'But it was all OK. No one dead.' She contemplated a few seconds, then added, 'I got Bessie to wash her hair. Did you know she was not allowed shampoo? I cut her hair for her. Didn't do a bad job either. And phoned the dentist and got her an appointment... I was thinking I could use her. But those teeth.' She grimaced. 'And her clothes. Some that fit properly, some colour and design. I don't know what she wears for underwear.'

He said, 'At least someone is benefiting from our shenanigans.'

She put a hand on his.

'Don't be so jumpy, Jack.'

'Lack of sleep,' he said with a brief smile. 'Got back home and just couldn't sleep. I was thinking of going out and buying some booze... That would have been disaster. So I phoned you.'

'You're safe here.' She squeezed his hand.

'I kept thinking of everything that could go wrong,' he said. 'The things you don't think of.'

'You buried him deep in the forest,' she said.

'We did,' he said, seeing the woodland site in memory's cinema. 'A good three feet down.'

'And why should that be disturbed?'

He couldn't think why. Too deep for dogs, deer don't dig. Off the main drag... They didn't speak for a little while, both contemplating the remote possibility of discovery.

At last, she said, 'I'm sorry I was sniffy about the sofa, the one you bought.' She shook her hands. 'It's fine. Clean. It'll fill the space and I'll get some covers for it.'

'It has nothing of him on it.'

'The whole point of it,' she said. 'I was stupid. Wanting something pitch perfect – when all that really mattered was getting rid of that one. And the new one will do. Fuck high design. A sofa is to sit on. I'll make something of it. You wait.'

He wanted her closer. She seemed such a long way off. So far to travel, that yard.

She said, 'I wish that skip would go. The carpet's in it. And my dress.' She bit her lip. 'Although it's deep down.'

'The skip goes tomorrow,' he said.

'And what happens to it?'

'It is emptied into landfill.'

'And then what happens?'

He felt she was teasing him, inviting him, the way she was gazing at him.

'A bulldozer comes along and compacts it.'

'And then what?'

'The rubbish gets buried under more rubbish. And the bulldozer compacts it still more.'

He crossed no man's land. The yard. And they embraced. Flesh grasped flesh. Tiredness, guilt and fear found solace. They were here, they were alive, nothing would happen where they were together.

'Let's go to bed,' she said.

'I'd best phone Mia first. Or she'll just phone me.'

She rose, returned for a quick kiss on his forehead, and said, 'I'll be waiting for you.'

And she left him.

He felt warm, needed. How glad he was that he'd come. He shuddered at what he might've done if left to himself. All those shops, all those bottles, all those perfectly legal knockout drops. And had a vision of himself at home in a drunken stupor. And the hell of those times.

Drowning the day. To wake up to vomit and diarrhoea. And a pounding head that said only more drink can make this bearable.

He phoned Mia.

She talked telescopes; she'd been researching them on the internet. And wondered whether he might add something to her mother's promised £500. He said he'd consider it. A safe, not today answer. She asked him about his day. He told her it was boring, just building work. Knocking down a wall, putting up a fence. Nothing much.

'How did your dinner go with that woman?' she said.

He'd forgotten she knew.

'Quite well,' he said carefully. 'We're getting to know each other.'

'Is she special?' she said.

'I don't know yet.'

'When will you know?'

He thought for a moment then said, 'It's like making friends. You're around them a while, and suddenly you know. Or perhaps you think – I actually don't like this person very much. I don't know which way it's going to go.'

'I know what you mean,' said Mia.

A little more telescope talk followed, thoughts on Brighton and hopes for the day away on Saturday. And then goodbyes.

Jack was glad it was done, the phone call. He hated lying to her. Telling her he was working today when it was a write off. And sins of omission too, the early morning journey, he thought as he headed for the bathroom. And looked at his deadened eyes in the mirror as he cleaned his teeth. He washed, soaped his hands thoroughly, bathed his face in warm water with her flannel. It would take more than soap to clear this away. He wiped himself and went to the bedroom.

Anne was under the duvet, fast asleep.

Chapter 44

Nancy was in bed listening to the radio. It was a programme she really liked, Big Band Days. Music from the 30s and 40s. Her time. Glenn Miller, Frank Sinatra when he was young, Vera Lynn, the Forces' Sweetheart. Sweeping music, songs of love and longing, all before that rock'n'roll swept it away with its loud, harsh beat.

John had liked this sort of music too. They'd listen together in the evenings, she with a puzzle magazine, he with one of his model narrowboats, the bits all over the table. They'd argued about him taking up all the table. And finally agreed, after a monster row when they didn't talk for two days, that he'd use the shed during the day, then after dinner he could use the table, but had to clear it all away last thing.

Mostly they'd agree about things. Some rows, some sulks. Some for days. They'd got better as they got older, avoiding the touchy spots.

She was worried about Bessie. She was spending too much time with Anne. Was that the way it was going to go, now the girl's father was out of the way? She'd run in, run out, empty the cat litter and away she'd go. Downstairs to her new friend.

And she hadn't come this evening like she said she would. Was she down with Anne again? Bessie had hardly known Anne before today. And now it was like best friends. Just like that. Anne had cut and washed her hair. And Nancy had to admit, it was a considerable improvement. She looked less like a washerwoman, more like her age.

She liked their afternoons together, Bessie making the tea. Biscuits and talking. Were they to go? But one thing she did have. Tickles. Bessie would come for him, if not his mistress.

Though she could say, no – you can't see him. Then see how she liked it, being shut out. Except it wouldn't work. Who would do her shopping, change the cat litter? She had no threats.

Growing old was terrible. You needed people so much, but they didn't need you.

A Glenn Miller medley was playing. All that big band stuff, the trumpets swelling. She remembered going to an American dance during the war. Her mother thought she was at the pictures. It was the first time she'd seen jiving. Such wild dancing. It was quite shocking. And exciting.

What was happening upstairs? The bedsprings hammering again. That all should have stopped with her father gone. Was she jumping on the bed? She didn't like it. It wasn't neighbourly. She'd tell her tomorrow.

If Anne didn't keep her all day.

Chapter 45

Bert smelt the dress, the perfume lingering in it, a slight tang of sweat in the armpits. It conjured up the fullness of the woman wearing it. Her breasts, her bare shoulders. It was short. Her legs, the top of her thighs and buttocks. He laid it out on the seat beside him, a sexy red thing, torn at the neckline as if someone was trying to get at her tits. Frank? And blood, spattered and dried over the front.

He'd had to work hard getting it out of the skip. It was way down, barely visible. Bert had to lift out some of the bricks and almost climb in to pull out the carrier bag. He didn't immediately look inside, beyond a glance, as there was a woman watching from the house. Let her watch. What was thrown away was thrown away.

He put the bricks back in the skip like a good citizen, and took his booty to his car parked across the road. It was a sexy thing, almost tarty. The shortness, the low cut neck. The sort of thing they wore to tease. And maybe Frank got fed up with being teased... Might that be the tale of this dress? Frank's blood, when hubby came back to find him at it.

There was a tap on his window.

It was the woman who'd been watching him. He let the window down. The dress was beside him laid out, he knew she could see it. So what?

She said, 'Excuse me, but are you a friend of Frank's?'

'Yes, I am,' he said carefully.

She was quite a nice looker, bending half over to talk.

'I haven't seen him the last couple of days,' she said. 'And his car is always out here. I usually see him drive off in the mornings... Do you know where he is?'

He ignored the question. 'You a friend of his too?'

'Well,' she shrugged, 'a neighbour, sort of friend. He comes down from time to time for a coffee. He's a nice man, always friendly.'

Bert knew why his mate was friendly with her. Who wouldn't be?

'I can't speak now,' she said. 'I've got children coming any minute. But if you can come back after ten o'clock then we can put our heads together... Bessie, you know, Frank's daughter, can look after the kids for a bit.'

He thought, yes, he'd like to put his head together with hers.

'Sure, I'll drop in later.'

'My name's Anne,' she said. 'Flat 1.'

She held her hand out. He shook it and held it a little too long.

'Bert,' he said. 'I look forward to a coffee.'

She indicated a car that had pulled up. 'There's my first children. Must go. See you later, Bert.'

And with a parting smile, gave a wave, and crossed the road. He continued watching as she spoke a few words to the young, plumpish woman who was getting out of the car. Somewhat obscured by the car, he saw the two of them getting two small children out and onto the pavement. They each held the hand of a child and led them up the path, up the few steps and into the house. The door closed on them.

A friend of Frank. Well, Frank had a secret life then. Couldn't blame him for that. A coffee offered. You never know what else. They were already on speaking terms. And had an important topic of conversation. You never know.

He'd have to ask Bessie about her. In fact, might even call on her in a while. Last night was alright. He'd stayed until about ten, when he'd had his fill. He didn't take the second steak with him but had left it as he thought he might well come back tonight. Fill the inner man, so to speak.

The day was looking up.

Warm for the time of year, a sky of fast, broken cloud, the sun coming through every so often. Bert kept his window down. Must clear up this wagon. Never know when it might have a passenger. He'd get Bessie on it later.

A car drew up opposite and a woman carried a baby to the house and rang the bell. Anne opened up. She took the baby and the woman left hurriedly. Within a minute she'd driven away.

Bert looked at his watch. Gone nine. He had the morning off. Just the morning. He had to be in the shop by two, then working late till seven. He could be over here by eight thirty, the steak on the table. Depending what happened in Flat 1 of course.

A black man and a pregnant white woman came out of the house. Yes, they were the ones. And it was her, definitely her, who he'd seen yesterday prodding down in the skip. And he, the black man with the briefcase. Though no briefcase today and no suit either. Both in anoraks. The same two from upstairs who'd been rowing about events in the forest.

Didn't Frank say she was a teacher? They got in before school started. Not today, though. And he didn't look like he was going to work either. Bert watched them get in a car a little way along the roadway. And when they drove off, he let them get a little way ahead, and followed.

Chapter 46

A good night's sleep changes the world. He'd woken in the early hours, Anne had woken too. A flurry of sex and he'd slept till the alarm went off at seven thirty. No journey to work, and with a shower and breakfast, he was set up for a day's work. And needed to be, with yesterday nothing but the van crash.

So stupid. So quick. And all the money it would cost him to put right. Two hundred, and up would go his insurance on top. At least there was no injury involved. Forget it. Except it kept coming back to taunt him. The quicker he got the van done the better.

Work.

There were seven concrete pillars to go in. Each had grooves down its length on both sides. And the two metre wide sections of fencing, made up of wooden slats joined to a wooden post at either end, would be held in place by the grooves. Simple enough, a question of getting the spacing right. Measuring and lining up as you go.

Jack laid a string line along the length where the wall had been. The brickwork had been taken out to earth-level. The rest could stay, except where the posts needed to go in. There, any subsurface bricks would have to come out so he could dig a hole for a post.

Should be straightforward.

He'd left his tools in the shed overnight, thank goodness, considering the condition of his van. Just by luck, he had everything here this morning.

He'd cemented the first post in, when the skip lorry arrived. He heard the hydraulics from the garden and went out to check. Jack gave the driver the thumbs up. It was the same man who'd taken the last skip away. Jack watched him attach the chains and haul the skip onto the back of the lorry. He stayed to watch it be driven off.

Straight to landfill, and good riddance. He felt a relief at that. The evidence buried and bulldozed in with more loads day by day. It was simply a question of keeping mum.

He had a second post cemented in, with the fencing slotted between them, when Anne invited him in for a coffee. Jack took his boots off at the French windows, they were splattered with cement and the soles clagged with soil from the flower bed.

In the nursery, Bessie was handing the children their milk and slices of apple. He greeted her, and saw at once she had a bruise on the side of her face.

'How'd you do that, Bessie?'

'I bumped into the door,' she said.

He frowned, not believing her, but didn't press it.

'I'm trying to keep off your plants,' he said.

'Thank you, Jack.'

He went in to the kitchen where Anne was making toast, two coffees already on the table. Jack sat down and sipped a coffee.

'What d'you make of Bessie's face?' he said.

Anne sat down opposite. 'She had a visitor last night,' she said. 'A chap called Bert. A friend of Frank's.'

'He would be.'

'He had a dinner appointment with Frank. Was pissed off when he didn't come home.'

'And took it out on poor Bessie.'

'More or less,' said Anne.

'I'm not having that,' said Jack. 'I'll see him off.'

Anne held up a hand. 'Don't, Jack. He might be suspicious.'

'He can't take squatter's rights!' seethed Jack.

'Don't have a go at me. I didn't do it.'

The toast popped from the toaster and she rose to take

the slices out. She put them on a plate in front of Jack.

'I've arranged to talk to him later,' she said. 'I'll make it clear we're keeping an eye on him.'

'If I see him, I'll knock his teeth out one by one with a cold chisel.'

'Jack!'

He nodded at her placatingly, not wanting to get into an argument with her. Instead he concentrated on spreading marge and marmalade on his toast. They didn't talk for a while. Jack was cooling his temper, Bessie was vulnerable – but he had no right taking it out on Anne.

'Take it step by step,' she said. 'I'll talk to him... Then we can decide what else we might do.'

'OK,' he said, corking his aggression.

She asked him about his daughter. He knew it was displacement activity, but it was fine. He told her about the trip to Brighton en famille tomorrow. And the bribery offered to Mia. They chatted safely about families, about the problems of moving, until Jack thought it time to get back to work.

Back to digging, making cement, putting posts in. He knew what he was doing, how to line up and mix cement. And there were no other human beings to screw things up.

Chapter 47

The road went through the forest, with woodland either side. It was almost empty of traffic, so Bert could keep a fair way back and keep them in sight. He drove steadily, hoping they wouldn't do a sudden turn off where he might lose them.

It was when passing a car park that he caught a glance of a single car in it. Orange, could it be an Aurora? Frank's? Could well be, with all the talk of forests. What was his car number? BEC something. He was past it, couldn't stop to check as they were driving straight on. Later, he'd come back and see.

Had Frank been killed here? Or, he grasped at an alternative, back home and driven here in his own car, to get it off his doorstep. Bound to be found though, sooner or later. If it was him doing it, he'd take off the number plates and torch it.

These amateurs.

Not much further on, they turned off into a car park. He drove past, unsure what to do. They didn't know him, but he was hanging around their house and they might at some time connect him. Dare he park in the same place? He'd chance it. A hundred or so metres up the road, he did a u-turn, and drove back to the car park and pulled in.

They had the doors of their car wide open and were taking off their shoes and putting on walking boots. This hadn't occurred to him, that it might be muddy in the forest. He was wearing trainers; well, he'd suffer wet feet if it came to it. He saw they were looking at him, and got out his thermos and poured himself a cup of tea, making it look like he had some purpose in his halt.

He was perhaps 20 metres away, and turned his mirror so he could see them without looking in their direction. They wore woolly hats and had backpacks. As they tied their walking boots, he wondered whether he might have this wrong. Maybe they were simply going for a hike in the forest. Surely not? Two of them taking a weekday off, especially a teacher – didn't make sense. They were just trying to make it look right.

But he still had a niggling doubt, as they headed into the forest from a narrow path on the edge of the car park. He gave them half a minute, locked up his vehicle and followed. They were walking slowly; he could hear them talking, not the words but the murmur of them.

About half the leaves had fallen from the trees, with lots of cloudy sky visible between the branches. The ground was dampish, in places churned up by boots, tyre tracks and horses. He couldn't avoid going through watery mud, and quite soon his feet were cold and wet. He hoped this wasn't a waste of time.

On a straight section of path, he hid behind a tree and watched his quarry. They were searching the ground, she one side, he the other. Clearly looking for something. Their row last night, didn't keys come into it? Keys so important that both of them had taken a day off to find them.

This wouldn't be a waste of time.

He'd have liked to hear their conversation but daren't get that close. With the leaf-fall, they might hear him. So he kept back, keeping to their pace, avoiding piles of leaves, walking when he could hear them walking. Stopping when he couldn't.

Bert found the keys. He might not have done if he hadn't stepped on them under a leaf and felt them through his trainers. There were four keys, the fob was a sort of flag. Nigeria it had written underneath, a Nigerian flag then.

Excited at the find, he wrapped them in a tissue and thought of heading back as he'd got what they'd come for.

They were going to be very disappointed. Maybe have another row. But he needed to know where they were going. Logic told him that on a visit to the woods, in the last day or so, they had dropped the keys. Most people would have duplicates, might be annoyed at having to have more cut. But they wouldn't take a day off work, and come all this way to search for them.

Both of them.

He knew, as he'd half known before he'd set out, Frank was buried out here.

Chapter 48

Third post in, and two sections of fencing slotted between them. Jack stood back to look at his handiwork. Good, with the posts plumbed upright. This was the first time he'd put this sort of fencing in, but it was all going smoothly. He was about to prepare the cement for the fourth post when he realised he hadn't enough. He had bought three bags and was using half a bag for each post. He obviously couldn't count to seven.

If he'd had his van, he'd just have popped out and bought an extra. As it was, he had a bag and a half left for the remaining four posts. If he put a bit more ballast in each hole, a little less cement – it'd work. Better get his sums right this time. He did a quick scratch in his notebook and figured it. Three eighths of a bag each. He checked. Yep. Awkward amount.

He poured a quarter, roughly, out of the open bag and put it in a bucket. He opened the last bag and took a quarter of that and poured that in, giving him three eighths of a bag in the bucket. Sums! The bucket would do for one, then the small bagful for another and the other bag divided in two. That would give him the same for each. He was quite pleased with his working out. Fractions n'all.

Of course, if he'd noticed he was short first thing, then he could have taken a bit from all three bags to make up the last. But at least he'd spotted it before it got too bad.

Bessie came out from the nursery. She went over to the part of her flowerbed where Jack had put in the first posts and fencing.

'Not too bad, is it?' he said.

'No, not bad at all.'

And he was aware from the way she was looking that they were talking at cross purposes. He was referring to his fencing work, and she to her flower bed. It wasn't worth picking her up on it, if they were both happy. Though her bruised face, that left him far from happy. He stuck his shovel in the soil.

'Bert came last night, didn't he?'

'Yes,' she said. 'He came to see Dad. He brought a couple of steaks for them.'

'You cooked him one?' he said.

She shrugged. 'Yes.'

'Just for him?' he went on.

'I didn't want one anyway.'

'Why did he hit you?'

She was looking down at the ground, shuffling her feet.

'Because, just because...' She was rubbing her hands feverishly. 'Because Dad wasn't there. Because I didn't know where he was. Because...' She stopped and turned her back on him.

He put a hand on her shoulder.

'Did he rape you?'

She didn't reply and he knew the answer.

He said, 'We'll sort this out, Bessie.'

She shook his hand off her shoulder, took a couple of steps away from him and turned round. There were tears on her face which she rubbed off with her sleeve.

'I thought with Dad gone it would be over,' she said with a sniff, 'but it's all starting again.'

He took a step towards her, shaking his head. 'Oh Bessie.'

'Do you know what he said?' she exclaimed.

'No,' he said helplessly.

'Just as he was getting dressed he said... this'd be a good place to move into.'

'I won't let him,' said Jack.

'You'll be gone,' she exclaimed, her whole body pushed forward in declaration. 'But I'll be here and he knows I'll be here.'

She turned, and ran across the grass and through the French windows.

Chapter 49

Maggie stepped out of the forest and onto the hardened clay of the car park. Hers was the only car present. There'd been another earlier when they arrived, and the man had seemed to be watching them. Probably just her nervousness. You think everyone is watching you, when really it's you watching them. David caught her up.

'What a waste of time,' he said.

'At least we know,' she said wearily, 'they're not clearly visible.'

'To us,' said David.

'Do you want to go look again?'

David sighed. 'We've been here more than two hours.'

She put a hand on his shoulder. 'Are you sure you dropped them here?'

He groaned. 'Practically sure.'

'So they just could be somewhere else. Could be?'

'I don't know where else,' he said weakly.

She bit a finger. 'We've scoured the grave area. Round and round that half a dozen times. Up and down the path twice...'

'I feel so damned stupid,' he said. 'What on earth are we doing here, Maggie? It's not as if we've killed anyone.'

'Just carted a body into the forest and buried it,' she said archly.

'Fuck off,' he said.

'Fuck off yourself.'

'Let's find a café and get a bite to eat,' he said. 'Talk it over there.'

'OK.'

She patted him on the arm and they crossed to the car.

She went round to the driver's side.

'Bugger!' she exclaimed. 'The window's smashed in.'

He came round to see. The driver's side window was broken. There was glass on the seat and floor.

She opened the doors.

'Anything missing?' he said.

Maggie looked around inside, opened the compartments, then searched her pockets. Then searched them again.

'What's up?' he said.

'My phone's gone.'

Chapter 50

Bert was triumphant. A classic morning. And to top it all, here he was with Anne. Smart, classy, and in her sitting room. She'd gone off to make them coffee. Was she giving him the come on? No wrong moves, this was worth a bit of patience.

He rubbed his hands. He knew where Frank was buried. The couple had gone round and round that area, searching. He'd managed to sneak in closer to hear them talking. And got the gist of it, the burying in the night. He noted the T carved on the tree. Why T? It didn't matter why. Just where.

That place, the clearing, his old mucker was buried.

And he'd left them, still searching for what he had in his pocket. At the car park, he looked in her car, knew they were in the forest and would be there for a while yet, there was no one about. So he'd smashed in the car window and taken her phone. Fancy leaving what must be 400 quid's worth of phone in your car. And she a teacher, for God's sake.

And could you credit it! He'd tried several pin numbers to get in. And hers was 4321. Why bother with a pin – if that is all you're going to do? He pitied her poor kids.

Then he'd driven to the other car park. And it was Frank's car alright. The first three letters, BEC in the number plate. His orange Aurora. Obvious it had been there a couple of days from the leaves around and on top. He'd looked inside. It had been cleaned up. And so he made sure not to touch it. No way was he going to leave his prints.

A classic morning.

Anne returned holding a tray with two coffees and a plate of biscuits. She put it down on the low table and handed him a coffee.

'Help yourself to biscuits, Bert.'

'Thank you, Anne.'

He liked saying her name. Best mates already.

She said, 'I haven't seen Frank for a few days. His car hasn't been around... I'm a bit worried.'

He said, 'It's good to have concerned neighbours.'

He sipped his coffee and crunched a ginger biscuit.

'We always had a chat, most days,' she said. 'He had strong views. He was disturbed about the state of this country. All the immigration... And I must say I tend to agree. You catch a bus – and you hardly hear any English spoken. The Queens Market is all Asian and West Indian...'

'Eastern Europeans catching up fast,' said Bert.

'Why do we let them all in, Bert?'

'Soft government,' he said. 'They want cheap labour. Except half of them are on the scrounge. Out to get what benefits they can and make use of the health service. HIV tourists.'

'Oh!' said Anne, throwing her hands up, 'I went to the doctor the other day, and the waiting room...'

'I bet.'

'I swear I was the only English person there.'

'Typical of the state of this country,' said Bert. 'It's no good pussy footing. You have to get tough if you want to sort it out. Frank knows that.' He was careful with his tense.

'He does.'

She passed him the biscuits. He took one in silver paper.

'Any idea where he is?' she added.

'I know where he is, Anne.'

Her attention roused him. Had she just put on lipstick while making coffee? For him.

'Where?' she said.

He sucked his lower lip, considering, then said, 'He's dead.'

'My God!' she exclaimed throwing up her hands. 'How can you know that? An accident or what?'

'No accident,' he said. Loving how he was her total focus.

'You're not suggesting murder?' her hand on his arm. 'Whoever would do such a thing?'

Bert tapped his nose. 'Who'd you think?'

Anne leaned back on the sofa. She cupped her chin. 'Who? You're implying I might know.' Then flicked her fingers. 'He had a fight with David upstairs. I was there.'

'Got it in one,' said Bert impressed.

'Him and his wife Maggie,' she exclaimed almost gleefully, 'they might've killed him then and there – if we hadn't been present. Frank was only speaking his mind, when David went wild. I was terrified.'

'They killed him,' he said. 'In this house maybe. Perhaps their flat. Then they took him to Epping Forest in his own car. Buried him. And dumped his car there.'

'How do you know all this, Bert?'

He smiled. She smiled back. Dare he make a play? No, show her he could be civilised. Drink coffee and biscuits. Accept the attention.

'I've been doing a bit of nosing.' He took a bite of biscuit, playing out his tale. 'I found her dress in the skip outside. Torn, blood on it. So obviously, there'd been a fight.' She was nodding, rapt. He sipped his coffee. 'I was at Bessie's last night, and heard the two of 'em upstairs having a row. So I crept up and listened in. And sort of pieced together what they'd been up to. They lost some keys in the forest when they were burying him. Had to get 'em back, didn't they?' He smirked at the thought of his triumph today and the woman who was now hanging on every word. 'I followed them this morning. Both took the day off work, they were that desperate, and drove out to the forest.'

'To find the keys?'

He nodded. 'They were searching all over the path. Went right in the forest to where he was buried. I heard 'em say so clear enough. Round and round searching. But they never were going to find them. Because I did.'

He took a small plastic bag out of his pocket and held them up.

'May I?' she said.

He handed them over. 'Don't take them out the bag.'

She examined them through the plastic. 'That one's the front door key to the house. I don't know the others. Nigerian flag on the fob.' Her hand went to her mouth. 'Must be his.'

'They're shitting themselves, I'm sure.'

'We should call the police,' she exclaimed. 'A couple of murderers in this house... They can't go unpunished.'

'They won't,' said Bert. 'I just want to make sure of it.' He shook the little bag, and took another bag out of his pocket containing a smart phone. 'I will tie 'em up so tight they'll get twenty years or more.'

Chapter 51

Jack entered the sitting room.

'What do you want, Jack?' said Anne sharply.

Bert slipped the phone and keys into his pocket.

'I want to talk to him. Bert.' He strode across the room, and stood over the back of the sofa where Bert was seated. 'You, mate. I want a word with you about Bessie.'

'Look, mate, I don't know who you are or what you want.' He was twisted round to look up at Jack. 'But I suggest you mind your own fucking business.'

'It's my business when you rape her!'

'The little cow is lying.'

Anne bit her lip. Jack would ruin everything.

'Please leave, Jack,' she said as calmly as she could. 'Bert is my guest. I will not have my guests insulted.'

He turned to her in amazement. 'He raped Bessie.'

'He said he didn't,' said Anne.

'And you believe him!' He pointed outwards. 'She is in your nursery, looking after your children – and you are calling her a liar!'

'I'd like you to leave, Jack.'

'And what about this rapist?'

'Fuck you, mate!' exclaimed Bert getting to his feet. 'I'll kill you for that.'

'Get out, Jack!' yelled Anne. She rose. She pushed him on the chest with both hands. 'This is my flat. I will not have you here insulting my guests.'

'He raped Bessie, I tell you!'

'I don't believe it. Now, leave. Or I'll call the police.'

'Oh, you will, will you?' he said with a short laugh. 'You'll call the police?'

'Shall I throw him out for you?' said Bert.

She was between the two, their mutual hatred incinerating the air.

'Please, no, Bert. This is my nursery. I don't want violence here.'

'Point taken,' said Bert contritely.

'Go, Jack. Leave, at once.' She gripped his arm firmly, and pointed out of the door. 'I will not have this gutter behaviour.'

'If I go, I won't be back.'

'Leave!' she yelled at him. 'You have no rights here. Go!'

Jack went to the door, where he turned and pointed at Bert.

'If you lay another finger on Bessie, I'll strangle you with my bare hands.'

And was gone.

For a while neither spoke, floored by the tornado that swept through the room, scattering everything.

'She's lying,' said Bert. 'How could she say such things?'

Anne nodded. 'I know she tells lies. About her dad too. It's disgusting.'

'And she convinced that prat. Is he your fella?'

'We had a short thing, if that's what you mean. And it's well and truly over, I'll tell you that. How dare he come in here and throw accusations around... How dare he!'

Bert suddenly grasped her. He kissed her. In the first instance, she resisted, and then accepted, hungrily.

Chapter 52

Jack dug as much soil as he could out of the hole. It wasn't wide enough. There were bricks in the ground on either side. He got down on his knees and attacked them with his cold chisel and club hammer, taking out the bits as they broke away.

He couldn't believe what had just happened. Anne had thrown him out, and was now having coffee and biscuits with that animal. They were on the sofa together. Flirting? He'd heard of women turned on by violent men. Sado-masochistic. Which made him wonder what really might have happened with Frank. Her damsel-in-distress tale of rape... Or was it a sex game gone wrong? Then there was her husband's death six years ago... All he'd heard was her side of the story.

He didn't know her at all.

He had simply been taken in by her helplessness, by sex of course. The old, old story. Put the body in a bag, run it up to Epping Forest. Buried it like a faithful dupe. Carted off her sofa. And now she had no further use for him.

What a player!

She was a childminder. In there with her toddlers, reading them stories, giving them their juice and slices of apple... That was her theatre. The other actors confirmed her. But what was she really?

Break bricks. Make holes for fence posts. That made sense. But the whys and wherefores of yesterday all rested on the foundation of her say-so.

Had he been taken for the biggest ride of his life?

What was she doing with that ape? Her next dupe? It hardly mattered to Jack. Sex and murder, he was out of it. Except of course, he wasn't. That folly of the other night bound him to her. Everything was now cleaned up; he'd fucking well cleaned it up for her. Her knight errant, her total fool, had got rid of her sofa for her, put her carpet in his skip. Everything that might implicate her, he had removed.

She could plant it on him.

His stupidity, his utter stupidity.

Except there were witnesses, weren't there? Bessie, Nancy, David and Maggie. But they were not witnesses; they had all turned up after the murder.

Such a mess! She was playing her own game. All he could do now was get the job done and get the hell out of here.

He put his hammer and chisel aside. The hole was big enough. The post lay on his wheelbarrow. Make up some more cement.

Bessie came out of the house. He watched her approach. She looked better with her hair done, but that shapeless overwashed dress... And the bruise on her face.

She said quietly, 'I heard you shouting.'

'Bert called you a liar.'

She seemed to shrivel, bit her lip. He knew she wasn't lying. And knew what he must do.

'You can't stay here, Bessie. Not with him around.'

She shrugged, her eyes wide. 'It's where I live. I haven't anywhere to go.'

He sighed, looking at the house, the open French windows on the ground floor, the brickwork and windows of the upper stories...

'I'm not leaving you here this weekend,' he said.

'What about Tickles?'

For a second or so, he tried to recall who she was on about. Right. The cat with the silly name.

'He can manage without you for a couple of days...' he said, though he knew it might be a lot longer.

'And what about Nancy?'

'You'd best go and see what shopping she needs for the weekend,' he said.

Chapter 53

Maggie was lying flat out on the sofa, her bare feet up on one arm, head resting on a cushion. She had showered when they'd got back, but was achy after their trek in the forest. David in an armchair was reading the Guardian, though much of it seemed not to his liking as he was simply turning pages, reading a few sentences and moving on.

'They're going to be awfully pissed off with me at work,' he said.

'I will have been deputised by some useless supply-teacher,' sighed Maggie. 'In they come with their box of tricks. The kids go wild. And they don't care because they are off at the end of the day. I won't make head or tail of what she's been doing with them... It's childminding really.'

'What are you going to do about your phone?'

She sighed, looking up at the ceiling as if there might be an answer there. 'Buggered if I know. Though I have to report it stolen for them to switch it off... He, I assume a he, could be phoning Africa or Tokyo and talking for hours. Bollocks. Do I have to inform the police?'

David put down the paper.

'When one loses 450 quid's worth of phone, one phones the police,' he said tartly.

'Thank you, darling, for your advice. Remind me never to ask for it again.'

'You just don't have to say it was in Epping Forest. Say it was around here in the street. How will they know?'

The landline rang.

As she went for the phone, she said, 'Food poisoning. I'd better groan if it's school.' She picked up the handset. 'Hello?'

'Is that Maggie Ayo...' said a male voice, attempting her full name.

'Ayodele,' she said helpfully. 'Yes, it is. How can I help you?'

'I've got your phone, darling.'

'I beg your pardon...' She signalled to David as she switched to speakerphone.

'I have your very handsome smart phone. Quite something.'

'You broke into my car,' she said.

'You're a stupid woman, leaving it in your car in an isolated car park.'

'I'm sure you haven't phoned me to call me stupid.'

'Almost as stupid as your husband, dropping his keys in the forest.'

David looked to her in alarm. She put a finger to her lips and tried to keep the fear out of her voice.

'My husband hasn't lost any keys,' she said.

'Oh yes he has. A Nigerian flag on the fob. I've got them here.' There was a sound which could have been jangling keys. 'Like I said, I found them in the forest.'

David was trembling, she wanted to scream, instead said, 'There's a reward for the phone... and for the keys.'

'I thought you said he hadn't lost any keys.'

'Maybe he has.'

'And maybe he buried a body, darling, and maybe you helped him, being a loving wife.'

She could barely breathe, fear clutching at her diaphragm.

'I don't know what you're talking about,' she managed to say. 'You've lost me.'

'T is for tits, T is for tub thumping lie, T is for two murdering arseholes.'

The phone went dead.

Maggie and David stared at each other. Words had evaporated. They were revealed naked in their sin.

'He knows,' she said at last. 'He has my phone, he has your keys. He knows.'

'Not quite,' said David. 'He thinks we murdered him.'

'Does that make any difference?'

'I don't know. I really don't know. But it means he doesn't know everything.'

'However did we get into this devilish business!' Her hands were pressing her forehead as if trying to push out the events. 'What possessed us to go burying bodies in the forest?'

'Neighbourliness.'

'It has to be blackmail,' she said. 'We are about to be stripped of every penny we've got.'

'No,' he said. 'We don't pay.'

'So what on earth do we do, David?'

'We bury the body somewhere else.'

'Oh no, I can't stand it. Will this never cease!'

She sank her face in her hands and wept.

PART FOUR:
IN THE FOREST

Chapter 54

They had a Chinese takeaway, though Jack ate most of it. He kept offering Bessie more but she wouldn't have it.

He had seen no other option but to take her to his place. No way could he ask Anne, and didn't trust her anyway. Nancy couldn't help, in fact it might be danger for Nancy herself. He had gone up to see Maggie and David and found them both pretty disturbed over something. He'd guessed it might be connected to recent events, but said nothing, not wanting to know. Maggie had obviously been crying, David was shaky. They said they couldn't help, were busy this weekend, family stuff.

And that left himself.

Of course, he could have left her at home, to the predations of Bert. But how could he? It was all such a tangle. He'd thought he was just burying a body to help Anne, simple, as if Frank could be just rubbed out and no one notice the space he'd been taking up. Except, sooner or later, Frank would have to be reported missing. And then there was Bert who was planning to take over Frank's flat and his daughter. Sure, Jack could change the locks, but that wouldn't keep him out. Besides which Bessie couldn't simply lock herself in day and night.

He'd told Bessie she could bring a suitcase. But she'd brought a carrier bag, and what was in it, Alison would have torn up for rags. He said nothing; she was not to blame for her poor wardrobe. Obviously, though, she needed new clothes, but Jack was out of his depth in that department.

Thoughts for tomorrow. Not tonight.

They walked to his place. Lucky he was working not far away. Next week, he must get his van fixed. He had some roofing work on and might have to hire a vehicle temporarily. More expense. He'd hoped to be finished today, but there were still two posts to go in. It had been harder digging the holes for the posts than he'd anticipated. Getting the remnants of wall out had slowed him up. Another day then. His tools were in the garden shed for the weekend. It didn't lock, but there was nothing valuable. Likely they'd be alright.

Finish Monday and head away.

'Can I watch television?' said Bessie.

'Of course,' he said. 'Whatever you want.'

She'd washed up. She'd insisted. There wasn't much with a takeaway. And she made them a cup of tea. He gave her his Daily Mirror and showed her the TV pages. And he read his Astronomy mag. There was a meteor shower next week. Be good if Mia were over, but he'd go out on his own otherwise...

His mobile rang.

'Hello,' he said.

'Hello, Jack.'

It was Anne. He went into the kitchen to talk.

'What do you want?' he said.

'I'd like to explain. Would you like to come over?'

'No.'

'Can I come over to your place?'

'No.'

'I need to explain, Jack. It's not like it seemed. I'm sorry I was so horrible. But I can't talk about it over the phone... Please let me come over.'

'I don't want to see you,' he said.

'Please, Jack. I had to do what I did. Let me come over.'

'You don't seem to be understanding me, Anne. Try listening. I don't want to see you.'

'Then how can I explain?'

'Write me a letter.'

And he hung up.

The phone rang again a few minutes later. It was the

same number. He cut it off. And again twice more. After that he switched off the ringtone.

And watched a romantic comedy with Bessie.

Chapter 55

It was a rainy morning, the sky charcoal grey, Nancy's windows snaky with drips, steaming up on the inside. Bessie would not come today. She had gone off with that builder for the weekend. He seemed alright... Nancy hoped he was. It just wouldn't be fair if he was to take advantage of her too.

First Bessie's father and then when he was gone, barely a couple of days, along comes that horrible man Bert. It was as if we were still living in caves and there was no law. But what was Anne doing with him? She'd seen her leave the house with him a little while ago, and go off in his car. Surely he hadn't stayed the night with her?

Some women are attracted to violent men. She could never understand it. Do they like their strength, being ordered what to do? Anne would learn soon enough when he hit her, like he'd already hit Bessie.

And then it would be too late.

She heard footsteps on the stairs, and hobbled across the room, to the window on her cane, in time to see Maggie and David going out. She watched them go down the path and out on the pavement to their car. And then drive away. She was the only one in the house.

No Bessie today, to have tea with and watch play with Tickles. She'd hardly seen Maggie for a couple of days. Everyone was so busy, except herself. She could write to Ted, she had a spare airmail letter. He said he enjoyed getting them, and had told her the last time he phoned that she was the only one he knew who still wrote letters. Perhaps she could phone him. Maybe later, there was a six hour time difference. They'd still be in bed.

She'd had her game of bingo at the church yesterday. That was quite pleasant. They came to collect her in a minivan. Tea and biscuits. Actually, she found bingo quite boring, but she liked the company. Nearly all old women. Widows like herself who married older men, and then lived on and on.

It broke up the week.

Tickles was asleep on the rug by the gas fire. She had the central heating on, but also the gas fire on low, as the mornings were getting cold these days. And she could hardly move until she'd got some warmth into her bones. Like a lizard on a rock, Bessie had said.

The girl had done some shopping for her yesterday. Bought her a couple of magazines, The People's Friend and a puzzle mag. She'd save them till later. It was going to be a television and reading day; she might not see anyone. Well, that was the way it was.

Days like this, she missed John. They might have argued from time to time, but he was there. Someone to cook for, to talk to. He could help her down the stairs and take her out to the park across the road. If he hadn't smoked all those cigarettes, he'd probably still be alive. Though who was to say what state he'd be in.

It's down, down, down as your body slowly gives up on you. No point complaining. That's the way it is. Nature.

She mustn't be miserable. There was no help for it; she was how she was. She was going to die one day, but it was no good moping and waiting for it to happen. Keep busy. She'd have a chat with Millie a bit later. First she needed to deal with the cat litter. No Bessie today.

Nancy couldn't get down to lift the tray, but she had a pair of tongs which she clipped to either side and lifted the tray onto a stool. She removed the tongs and poured the mucky litter into a carrier bag. Then put fresh litter in and with the tongs put it down on the ground again.

She was pleased with that. Clean litter for Tickles. The

trick was not to rush things. She could do quite a few things if she took her time.

Now she had to take it out to the bin. No rush. She put the carrier bag over her arm, took her stick and set off. She opened the flat door, left it open and began the journey down the stairs.

Take it slow. She could stop anytime she wanted.

At the ground floor she rested, sitting on the step. And thought it would be nice to have a chair down here, so she could sit down for a few minutes. She'd had one in her spare room; she'd get Bessie to bring it down on Monday.

Then she had a horrible thought. Suppose Bessie didn't come back. Suppose Social Services or whoever it was decided that this wasn't a safe place for Bessie? They might, they did things like that.

Maybe it was time for her to give up her flat too. Go into sheltered housing. There'd be people there to talk to, every day. But what a hullabaloo it was moving, packing everything. The very thought made her shiver.

But she could see it coming.

She opened the front door. It was teeming down, rain dripping off the roof of the portico, and she was only wearing slippers, hadn't bothered to put a coat on. Well, it wasn't far to the bin. A little wet wouldn't kill her. She came out of the portico into the rain. It was like having a shower, dripping onto her hair and down her neck. That quite tickled.

Off the steps and onto the ceramic tiles of the path. Careful here, they were slippery. No rush. Step by small step, hand on her stick, she made her way. Tickles had come out and was rubbing against her legs. He didn't seem to mind the rain either.

It was nice to be out, even to be a little cold and to have wet feet. Fresh air. She took a deep breath and then another. Her room could get quite stuffy with her keeping the windows shut.

She put the litter in the bin. That wasn't too bad. And turned about for the journey back.

Nancy had got to the bottom of the steps, when a gust of wind caught the front door and slammed it shut.

She knew she should've brought her keys out. Or for that matter put her shoes on, maybe her coat. Especially with no one in the house.

She climbed up the stairs, one by one, to the portico, one hand on the brickwork, the other on her stick. There, she tried pushing the front door. It was locked, of course. She rang the bells, although she was sure no one was in.

She was cold and wet. And frightened. She couldn't keep standing up, but she couldn't get down to the ground. Nancy went down a few steps, and then with some difficulty was able to sit on the wet steps. Her hands were going blue, she was breathless. She rested a minute, then worked her way backwards and up on her bum, step by step back to the portico. And there, seated, pulled herself out of the rain and against the side wall.

Her teeth were chattering. If she'd had a blanket, she'd have been alright waiting until someone came back. How long would they be?

Chapter 56

They parked in the forest car park where they'd left Frank's car. It was raining heavily as they left their own vehicle, wearing boots, putting their anorak hoods over their heads. Maggie had a cloth, and crossed to Frank's car. There, she put on gloves and began wiping the windows of the abandoned vehicle. David, also wearing gloves, had a small brush to remove the leaves and detritus that the bonnet, top, and rear had gathered in the few days that it had been left.

'We should take the number plates off and burn it,' said David.

'Not in this weather, dear.'

Both had backpacks. Maggie's was a day bag but David's a full rucksack out of which poked the handle of a spade.

'We can't come here every day or two to keep it clean,' he said.

She looked over her handiwork, the clean windows and handles. They would do. The car could have been newly parked by someone taking a forest walk in the pouring rain. A family row perhaps, or a sado-masochist.

'No, we can't leave it here,' she admitted. 'But one thing at a time.'

'Bloody weather,' said David, squirming in his collar.

'At least it keeps everyone else at home,' said Maggie.

David turned to his wife. 'We don't have to do this, you know.'

'I don't see any other way,' she said.

'Neither do I.' He kissed her on the cheek. 'Till death do us part.'

And they headed into the forest.

Chapter 57

Nancy was unconscious when they picked her up, splayed out in the portico. A passer-by in the street had spotted her lying there, and had come up to check. And then phoned the emergency services. They arrived in about fifteen minutes; two green clad paramedics who quickly assessed the situation. They wrapped Nancy in a blanket and stretchered her to the ambulance. And, with sirens blaring, were off to Newham General.

Once there, nursing staff took over. Her wet clothes were removed and she was wiped down before being put in hospital pyjamas. Nancy was still comatose and there was some concern about the level of her hypothermia. But, after an hour or so in the warmth, she began to wake. And it was quickly ascertained that although weak, she was in no danger.

They found her a bed. When told she would be staying for a few days, Nancy became agitated.

'My flat door is wide open. My cat will starve.' She wasn't sure which worried her most. 'The gas fire is on,' she exclaimed, giving her a third worry.

The nurse assured her someone would go round.

'But there's no one in!' she said, sitting up in bed as if about to leave, but then remembering she had only wet clothes and no key for the front door. Or any money or anything.

'We'll drop a note in,' said the nurse. 'And ask them to phone us to make sure everything is OK.'

Nancy sank back on the pillow. She couldn't do anything. Nothing had worked.

'I only went to take the cat litter out,' she said feebly.

Over the afternoon, she kept asking passing staff whether

anyone had closed her flat door and turned off the gas fire. She got variations on the same reply:

'We'll tell you as soon as we hear, Mrs Home.'

It wasn't until the evening that Maggie phoned the hospital. She'd seen the message dropped through the letter box with Nancy's concerns and with the hospital phone number. She told them she had switched off the fire, brought the cat in and closed the flat door. And had borrowed Nancy's keys to feed Tickles in the morning. She and David would visit Nancy in hospital tomorrow.

Nancy's relief was enormous. She knew in its way it was trivial. But it was all she had, her flat and her cat. The thought of the door open and the fire on had kept her in panic. It was such a weight off her mind that the fire was now off and the door closed. And Tickles would be fed. She trusted Maggie absolutely. Well, a teacher, and she'd fed Tickles before when she went on holiday with Millie in the summer. Or rather Maggie and Bessie had, but Bessie she couldn't quite trust then because her father took priority. And now there was Anne and that horrible Bert.

She must buy Maggie and David a present. Something for the baby perhaps.

Nancy ate most of her dinner, her first proper meal of the day. She drank a cup of tea too. And slept.

Chapter 58

Anne and Bert kept to the forest path, trying to avoid the deeper puddles and the growing muddy patches. There was no let up of the rain, striking the remaining leaves and painting the tree trunks. After a few minutes, they were barely aware of the background beat on the canopy and soggy undergrowth.

She wore her bright red Wellington boots and a smart blue raincoat over jeans. On her head she had a green and orange woolly hat. She'd brought her umbrella, and wondered whether it was worth the trouble, as it kept catching in the lower branches. Bert was hatless, his brown jacket open to the rain, and on his back a small rucksack. The cold hardly affected him. He worked often enough in the cold store behind the shop, he said, and just got used to it.

Though he was concerned for her. Was it a good idea, her coming too?

'You didn't have to come,' he said, dropping back. 'Not that I'm not pleased you're here.'

'I want to know where they buried him,' she said. 'He deserves more respect.'

Bert understood that. He was one for family funerals, always bringing flowers. And was a regular visitor to the local cemetery where his grandparents were buried, making sure the grave was kept up. On every visit he would weed and water the plants.

'We could've done it tomorrow,' he said, 'just as easily.'

She smiled at him. 'We're here now.'

'Nice coat you got there. Sorry it has to get so wet.'

She shrugged. 'It's a raincoat, Bert. That's what it's for.'

He liked her colours, the brightness of her. He was conventional when it came to clothes. A couple of snappy suits but the rest of his wardrobe was functional. But she obviously chose her clothing, had fashion sense. All of which kept him somewhat in awe of her, and he was surprised that she'd let him stay the night. Though not at first, earlier she'd sent him off, saying when she knew him better – which was fair enough. But then he'd phoned quite late, just to confirm today really, and she'd invited him over.

And was she something! The classiest he'd ever had. Sometimes when a woman took her clothes off, his first thought was she was better off dressed. Not Anne, she had the body, clothed or naked.

He was somewhat pissed when he first arrived, which showed in his performance, but he'd made up for it in the morning. She was a real goer. And they had a lot in common. She'd agreed to come along to England First in the week. Quite a trophy to enter the hall with on his arm. He was looking forward to that. They'd all be agog. Have to make sure they keep their hands off. Respect his woman.

He stopped, turned and stared about him through the mist of rain, as if daring the wet tree trunks to challenge them.

'What's up?' she said.

'Just checking,' he said. 'We don't want to be seen. But there's no one about. Who would be, this weather?'

He touched her face and wiped a drip down her cheek.

'We should go out for a meal this evening, Bert,' she said. 'A steak house.'

'Sounds great. Get this business done with. Celebrate.'

They continued, but now off the path. Bert led, she was his squaw, three paces behind. His ginger hair a mass of bejewelled droplets, pale hands by his side, a bluish tinge. On through wet bramble which soaked their leggings, over fallen trees. He was leader of the gang. On a promise.

In a clearing, he stopped.

'This is it,' he said.

'Where?'

He took a few steps to the side and pointed out an area. 'Under there. That's Frank's grave.'

She bowed her head and held her hands together against her chest. 'Rest in peace, Frank.'

'Amen.'

They stood a short while in silent prayer. He appreciated this in her, her seriousness. The way she made him aware who they were doing this for.

A mate had to be a mate.

Bert took off his backpack and put on a thin pair of gloves. Back to business. From his pack he took out the smart phone. And looked about the area, biting his lip thoughtfully.

'Just here,' he said, having decided on his stage management.

And pressed the phone a little way into the earth.

He took out the plastic bag containing the keys. He removed them and contemplated the ground.

'Here, I think.'

It was maybe ten feet from the phone. He pressed the bunch into the earth with just a tip of key showing.

'They don't need to be obvious,' he said. 'They'll dig the whole area over. The phone will do her, the keys him.'

'And when they come to the house,' she said, 'I'll give them the dress.'

'Yeh.' He smiled at her. That's what they'd worked out.

'Say I found it in the shed.'

He blew her a kiss. 'Nearly done, love.'

Out of his bag he drew a phone, a cheap one he'd bought this morning. He only intended making one call on it and then he'd chuck it in the canal. And then he took out his GPS tracker.

'All we need do now, to get this on the move,' he said, 'is phone the cops. Tell them there's been a murder, give them the co-ordinates of the grave and we skedaddle. You said that you'd talk to them? You got a better voice than me.'

'Yes,' she said, 'I'm happy to. To get those bastards.'

He stretched out to her with the new phone. She came over to get it from him. Took it and came into his arms which folded around her and they kissed, long lasting, under the rain, over the grave, cold and warmth mingling, a shared vengeance...

And the knife slid into his kidneys. Slid out, and came in again.

Anne backed away as Bert collapsed with a gasp, sinking to his knees, for an instant pointing at her, and then falling face first into the wet ground. Over him was David, holding a bloody kitchen knife. Maggie ran in from behind a tree, swiftly gathering up the smart phone and the keys.

Over the next hour, they opened Frank's grave. The earth was relatively soft, the digging not difficult in the loosened ground. David did most of it, Anne took over in his breaks. Maggie had a large thermos of coffee and chocolate biscuits that she shared around.

The soil off, there lay the bag, the corpse inside liquid and bloated. They spent little time looking but dragged Bert in. David trod him down further, laying an arm over Frank.

And earth was thrown over the pair.

Chapter 59

Brighton had evaded the rain, as if the West Sussex border was the precipitation limit. On the train down they remarked on the sunshine after their wet start. It was warm enough for Jack and Mia to be sitting on the stony beach, jackets still on but unzipped. The tide was coming in, the sea about ten metres away. Mesmerised, they watched the waves rear up, hit the shore and slide back.

'You could always have another go, Dad.'

'No. Firstly, she's interested in someone else. Secondly,' he hesitated and gave a short laugh, 'she's too much trouble.'

'You mean expensive?' said Mia.

'Sort of,' he said.

'You could tell her she's got to pay for herself.'

'I could. But I'm not going to.'

Mia threw a pebble. It landed close to the sea. She stood up and had another go. This time her stone landed in the rearing surf.

'Got there!' she said triumphantly and sat down again. 'I thought the beach would be sandy. How did all these pebbles get here?'

Jack contemplated. He hadn't really thought about it, though it was odd, a beach full of pebbles, when you came to think about it. As if they'd been tipped here by a giant lorry.

'I suppose they were rock once,' he said, 'and the sea pounded at it year after year...until it was broken up into pebbles.'

'But why no sand?'

This was pushing him to his knowledge limit.

'Well,' he said, 'sand is small enough to get washed away. Leaving the pebbles.'

This seemed to satisfy her, and just as well, because he was wondering why sand got washed away in some places but not others.

He said, 'We should get a book on it. Find out how the sea makes beaches.'

He knew it was all about time, that much anyway. The constant washing of the sea, the tides created by the gravity pull of the moon. Endless. And so rock becomes pebbles. He was a little surprised he could work it out. The universal forces, so obvious here. He was looking out to the far horizon, where the sky seemed to curve down like a rooftop to meet the sea.

'I'd like to live here,' he said.

'Why don't you?'

He shrugged. 'Money and work.'

She said, 'You couldn't really set up a telescope on this beach.'

'You probably could,' he said. 'You'd have to make it level. And stop it shifting on you.'

She screwed her nose up. 'A lot of trouble each time,' she said. Then added, 'If we get a garden...'

'South facing,' he interrupted, 'so you see the sun, moon and planets. And no tall trees blocking them out.'

'But she's talking about getting a flat,' sighed Mia.

'Then a south facing balcony,' he said. 'That'd be fine.'

'Yeh, a balcony,' she said, enthused. 'Could even leave the telescope out.'

'I wouldn't do that.'

'Maybe not. But I'd only have to carry it a short way...'

'You'll have to go house hunting with her. Make sure.'

'I will,' insisted Mia. 'Or she'll get something all wrong.'

There came a call from behind them.

'Jack! Mia!'

They turned to see Alison and Bessie coming down the slope of pebbles with plastic cups and a bag of something. But Bessie was the sight. He hardly recognised her in blue jeans and a yellow top showing through a green jacket.

'Smart!' exclaimed Mia, standing up to greet her.

'Do you like my new clothes, Jack?'

'They do wonders for you,' he said. 'You look a different person.'

'I'm so happy,' she said and she spun round.

Jack caught Alison's eye and they smiled at each other. And he wondered how much she'd paid. Though Alison was a canny buyer, and it was probably less than he thought.

Alison and Jack settled down for their coffees and the bag which contained donuts. Mia and Bessie left their coffees to cool and took their donuts to the sea edge, where they first threw stones and then took their shoes off to paddle.

'What are you going to do with her, Jack?'

'Take her back on Monday... And I'm not sure after that.'

'This man Bert...' she said.

'He's a monster,' he said. 'He's going to move into her flat if he's not stopped.'

'You need to take out an injunction on him,' said Alison.

'How do I do that?'

'Go and see a solicitor. I know a good one. I'll give you the contact details later.'

They were both watching Bessie and Mia who with rolled up jeans were in the surf, squealing at the cold.

He said, 'I've just enough work for the morning on Monday. So with luck I can see the solicitor in the afternoon.'

'Her dad's disappeared?' said Alison.

'Yes,' he said. 'And good riddance.'

'Might he come back?'

'I've a feeling not,' he said and changed the subject. 'She looks so much better in those clothes. What did you do with her dress?'

'Threw it away. And her underwear.' She stopped and looked at him. 'You're a nice guy sometimes, Jack.'

'Thank you.'

'But she can't stay with you.'

'No. That won't work. I'll have a chat with Maggie and David, Sunday night. See what they say. They're the couple up top I was telling you about. And go to the solicitor Monday afternoon, and hope we can sort something out.'

The waves beat on the beach, the sun shone. The two girls jumped and giggled in the surf, watched by two more reserved adults, drinking coffee and licking the sugar from the donuts off their fingers.

Thank you!

I am grateful to every reader who finishes one of my novels. I have taken you on a journey which I hope you have enjoyed. There are plenty of things you could have been doing, other than reading this book. So, thank you for your time.

If you liked **Jack of Spades**, here's what you can do next:

I'd appreciate a review on Amazon. In that way, you can help me tell other readers about my books. Without reviews authors get few sales on Amazon. So I'd be grateful for your review to help this series get on the move.

You can get a **FREE** ebook of **Jack of Spades** if you sign up for my readers' list. You may give it to a friend if you wish. Every month a lucky reader from the list will be sent a **free**, signed paperback of their choice from the series. Sign up using this link:

http://eepurl.com/buAh5H

When you sign up for my readers' list you will receive my regular newsletter. This will give you news about me, what I'm reading, tell you about my future books, PLUS a variety of giveaways.

Books by DH Smith

DH Smith is the name I use for my Jack of All Trades series. The books are all standalone novels and can be read in any order.

Out Now:
- Jack of All Trades
- Jack of Spades
- Jack o'Lantern

Coming Soon:
- Jack by the Hedge
- Jack in the Box
- Jack on the Tower

Books by Derek Smith

All my books, other than the Jack of All Trades series, are written under the name Derek Smith.

Mystery/Crime
Murder at Any Price

Fantasy
Hell's Chimney
The Prince's Shadow
Elektra

Other
Strikers of Hanbury Street (short stories)
Catching Up (poetry)

Young Adult Novels
Hard Cash
Half a Bike
Fast Food
Frances Fairweather Demon Striker!

Children's Novels
The Good Wolf
Feather Brains
Baker's Boy

For Younger Children
The Magical World of Lucy-Anne
Lucy-Anne's Changing Ways
Jack's Bus

About the Author

I live in Forest Gate in the East End of London. In my working life, I have been a plastics chemist, a gardener and a stage manager before becoming a professional writer. I began with plays, working with several theatre companies, and had a few plays on radio and TV, as well as on the stage. In the early 80s I became involved in running a co-operative bookshop and vegetarian café in Stratford, learning to cook, and having my first go at writing a novel. The first was a mess, and, after too many rewrites, binned. The transition from drama to novels took me a couple of years to get to grips with. My first success was a young adult novel, Hard Cash, published by Faber. Buoyed up by this, I stuck with children's work, did school visits, and made a hand to mouth living as a full time author, topped up with some evening class work in creative writing at City University and the Mary Ward Centre in Holborn. A few adult fiction titles appeared from time to time, between the children's list, and I have since been working more in that direction with my Jack of All Trades series.

My full name is Derek Howard Smith. I write as DH Smith for my Jack of All Trades series; all other books appear under Derek Smith. Earlham Books is my own imprint.

www.dereksmithwriter.com

45345794R00134

Made in the USA
Charleston, SC
21 August 2015